LILA FOX

EVERNIGHT PUBLISHING ®

www.evernightpublishing.com

DEVIL'S SONS MC: VOLUME ONE

Copyright© 2024

Lila Fox

ISBN: 978-0-3695-0997-0

Cover Artist: Jay Aheer

Editor: Audrey Bobak

LILA FOX

DEVIL'S FURY

Devil's Sons MC, 1

Lila Fox

Copyright © 2021

Chapter One

Amelia was startled when she was suddenly pulled aside as she came into the building she worked in. She tried to jerk her arm away until she saw it was her manager, Price.

"What?" she asked, concerned about the look on his face.

"I just heard about your dad and wanted to tell you I'm sorry."

She blinked several times to dispel the tears that gathered. God, she was so sick of feeling empty and sad. The last few years had been tough, with her father getting sick and then dying. Although it was expected to happen, and the nurse had even told her it would be soon, watching the life fade from her father's eyes made something inside her die.

She cleared her throat. "Thank you, Price."

"Does this mean you won't be working here too much longer? I know you took this job because you only had to work a few hours a night, two days a week, so you could be home to take care of him."

She exhaled and looked away for a moment. "I'll be here for another few weeks. I want to save up and make a new start somewhere else."

"You've given up a lot for your father."

"He was worth it."

"If you want to take the night off, I can have Candy take your shift."

"No, really. It will help take my mind off everything."

Price patted her shoulder. "Not many people would do what you did for a family member."

She hated that he was right. "Then they're fools."

"I wish I had a kid like you."

"You and Stacy won't have any kids?" Her manager and his wife were in their early thirties and still had time to have a family.

He snorted. "No. We decided early on our lifestyle wasn't meant for kids."

"I think you should reconsider. It's not the environment the child grows up in. It's their parents and how much they are loved."

Price smiled. "I'll talk to my wife. I think we'll regret it if we don't have at least one."

"I hope she agrees."

"Go on to the back and get ready. The place is already filling up."

She looked around the room and noticed more than half the tables around the stage were already filled with men. The two waitresses were rushing around, and the show hadn't even started.

As she passed by on her way to her own area,

Amelia waved at some of the women in the back behind the stage where they got dressed. Several women either ignored her or were outright hostile to her. She didn't know why and frankly didn't care. She was there for one reason, and it was to make money. Not friends.

It didn't take her any time to get dressed because the outfits were so damn skimpy. It was the makeup and wig that took forever to get on and looking right.

Tara plopped down in the chair beside her. "Hey, girl. I'm so sorry about your dad."

Amelia turned to her friend and accepted the hug and comfort.

Tara was the woman she'd connected with at the very beginning. They both had so much in common and felt the same way about the family. Tara had her mom at home that she took care of while Amelia was home with her dad. They both believed that family came first.

Tara was the one she would miss the most when she left.

Amelia wiped a tear from her cheek.

"So, are you leaving us?" Tara asked.

"God, I fucking hope so," one of the strippers, Sadie, said as she walked by.

Tara sneered at her. "Fuck off, skank. You're just jealous that the men like her and can barely stand you."

Sadie threw a hate-filled stare at Tara and Amelia. "Fuck you." Then she turned and stormed away.

"Well, she was pleasant like always," Tara said sarcastically, making Amelia laugh.

Amelia glanced at the doorway Sadie had left through. "I think she's just a very sad person."

"Of course you do, because you are a sweet person and find the good in everybody."

Amelia giggled at the disgust in her friend's tone. "First off, you're the same way, and secondly, you make it sound like a bad thing."

Tara shook her head. "Naw, I'm just afraid someone is going to take advantage of you in the future, and I won't be there to help. I worry about you, girl. You need someone to look after you."

Amelia squeezed her friend's hand. "I'll get by. I'm serious. I'll be fine. I worry about you too. You're stripping for the same reason I am."

"I know. It works the best for both our situations. Well, I hope you stay safe, and you know where I am if you ever need me."

"I wish you could come with me when I leave."

Tara shook her head. "I can't leave my mom."

"How is she?"

The despair on her friend's face saddened her.

Tara sighed. "The doctors think she's going to have to be put in a home that specializes in dementia. Mrs. Clark, who watches her while I work, can't handle her anymore, and I'm having a tough time getting her fed and watching her twenty-four hours a day."

Amelia's heart went out to her. At least her father had remembered her until the end. "I'm here for you."

Tara hugged her again. "I know. You're what makes my situation bearable."

"I'm glad. Now we have to hurry if we don't want to get yelled at."

Chapter Two

Fury, the prez of Devil's Sons MC, pulled up outside the strip joint, followed by several of his men. They were out to blow off some steam because Fury knew they'd all be fighting with each other to get the aggression out if he didn't turn their attention to something else. This was all because they'd just finished a long run and were glad to be home.

He also needed to look into finding new whores for them. They only had three left, and that wasn't enough for his men. He wasn't worried. Women flocked to them, and they got to pick and choose. Druggies and mommies weren't allowed. He didn't want to have to deal with either of them. Straight-up sluts were what he needed for his boys, and he was hoping he'd find some tonight.

After he got off his bike, he turned and rolled his eyes when he heard the guys arguing and pushing each other around. An ear-splitting whistle was all that was needed to get their attention.

"Burn and Ax, let's go."

Burn pushed Ax, making him laugh, which pissed Burn off some more.

"Fuck 'em," he told Traeger, vice-prez of the club and Fury's closest friend.

Traeger chuckled and followed him through the door.

Fury handed the doorman a couple hundred to get them all in. It was way above the amount they asked, but he was on good terms with Price, the manager, and he wanted to keep it that way.

He was used to the way people would take one look at them and move out of their way. It was good that they feared the club. It kept the citizens of Los Alamos, New Mexico, on their best behavior.

Very rarely was there a rape. It was one of his super peeves when men took advantage of women, and he went beyond rage if it was a child. Murders were close to nonexistent if you didn't count the ones they did. He smirked. Fortunately, the good people of Los Alamos didn't know that, and the people they killed were worse than the club.

He scanned the large room and saw that Traeger had already procured a few tables up in front. The men sitting at the tables gave them up freely and rushed to the other side of the stage, making him grin. He thought his vice-prez enjoyed scaring the hell out of people a little too much.

"Fury, I ordered a half-dozen pitchers for us."

Fury nodded at Ax. "Thanks, man."

"Oh, you're paying. I'm just doing the ordering."

Fury snorted. Fuck, he had said it was his treat tonight.

"Hey, I was hoping you guys would come in tonight," Price said as he came up to the tables and slapped Fury on the shoulder. "It's been a long time."

Fury turned his torso and shook Price's hand. "Yeah. We've been busy the last several months with construction on the compound. Then we had a run to make, but now we have some free time."

"I ran into Bear on Main Street, and he said it was a possibility you'd come. How's everything?"

"Good. The add-on to the clubhouse is done."

Price's eyes widened. "Jesus, I thought that would take you guys a year to build on. I saw it when I drove past the other day. It's bigger than the original club."

"We decided to spend money and our time with it. We all want comfortable and bigger rooms, and we soundproofed them, so we didn't have to listen to each other fuck. Since they had incentives wanting their own large bedrooms and bathrooms, they all kicked ass building it."

Price chuckled. "That probably did suck for the guys that had to share."

"It wasn't pleasant for anyone," Fury said with a growl, remembering some of the fights.

"Who gets the old rooms?"

"The toddlers…"

"What?" Price asked, confused.

"The prospects. Someone started calling them toddlers, and it stuck. Maybe because it's pissing the new guys off so much."

Price threw back his head and laughed. "Fuck, I can imagine."

Fury glanced at the stage when the next set started. The lights dimmed in the room, but they kept the stage bright. The music was a sultry, sexy tune. When he caught sight of the stripper, it was like his chest was hit with a tire iron. He was so stunned, he couldn't move or talk for a moment.

"Who the fuck is that?"

"That's Amelia. She goes by Cheri here. She hasn't been here a long time, and it sounds like she'll be moving on soon."

"Tell me about her," Fury demanded.

"I'll tell you the short version of her story. She got this job here so she could have the time and the money to take care of her father, who had cancer. He just died a few days ago. When I talked to her earlier, she said she would save up and go somewhere else. I wish she wouldn't. She's one of the guys' favorites."

He was unable to tear his eyes off her the whole time she danced. He could tell she wasn't an expert and hadn't done it long, and it made him smile. The way she moved was too jerky and part of a practiced routine, but it didn't matter to the men in the room. They went wild for her.

He guessed that her gaze stayed above the men's heads was because she didn't like what she did and hated the males' attention.

The crowd booed when she was done and went off the stage while another extremely thin woman slinked onto the stage. He could tell this one loved her job and craved the men's attention. She made sure of it with her provocative movements.

"I want to meet Amelia. Is she single?"

Price hesitated.

"What?"

"She's single, but she's not like the others, man. She's incredibly sweet and doesn't have a mean bone in her body. I don't think she'd ever agree to be a club slut."

Fury's eyes narrowed. "I don't like being questioned, Price, but I'll tell you because I know you care about her. She wouldn't be one of the whores. No other man would touch her."

"Seriously?" Price asked, and even Traeger turned in amazement.

"Will she come back out?"

"Yes. She has another two sets."

Fury stood. "Let me talk to her now."

Price led him to the backroom. Several women were naked, and it didn't bother them at all that he was back there. In fact, a few of them tried to get his attention. One little slut was so thin he could see her pelvic bone. She grabbed his arm, and he froze and looked down at her.

"Sadie, you don't want to push him," Price warned.

"I just wondered if he wanted a date." She tried to press her naked body to his.

He jerked her away from him and held her wrist tight. He enjoyed the gasp and the fear that filled her eyes.

"You don't ever touch me without permission. Do you understand?"

She nodded jerkily.

Fury knew it wasn't so much the words as the cold way he said it. He released her and followed Price.

Tucked back in a corner was a table with a big mirror and two girls sitting in front of it laughing.

"Hey, Amelia. I want you to meet someone."

Chapter Three

Fury had to bite the inside of his mouth to keep from laughing. Her gaze settled on him and moved up and down, and the more she saw, the bigger they got.

"Amelia, come here," Price said.

Both girls seemed frozen to their seats.

"Amelia, come here," Fury demanded in a dark raspy tone. That seemed to jolt her out of the trance she'd been in. The other woman jerked her gaze to Amelia and stood when she did. It looked like she wanted to protect her, but Price shook his head.

"He's not going to hurt her, Tara. I promise," Price told her.

Fury ignored them both because Amelia came to stand in front of him a few feet away and stopped.

"Closer," Fury murmured in a calm tone.

She did what he said and stood with her head bent back so that she could see his face.

"Jesus, you're a little bitty thing."

Amelia glanced at Price and seemed to relax a bit.

"My name is Fury."

She stared at him like he was an alien, and it made him chuckle. "That's a … different name," she whispered.

"It's my club name."

"Like one of those motorcycle clubs?"

"Yes. Exactly like that."

"I've never seen one up close."

Price snickered. "I told you."

Fury smiled. "I'm just a man, baby."

Amelia nodded. "Okay. What do you want with me?"

"I wanted to meet you."

"Why?"

He snorted. "Because I thought you were pretty, and I was wrong."

He watched his comment sink in, and a sad look filled her face.

"I know I'm not. I'm also bigger than every girl here, and no matter what I do, I can't lose weight. I—"

"Will you let me finish?" Fury chided.

She sighed, and then it looked like she braced herself for another insult.

"I don't think you're pretty, but gorgeous."

She snorted and shook her head.

He nodded. "I think you are. I love your curves, baby, and I will bet you the majority of men out there like them too."

"The other women look so much better in the outfits than I do."

"No. I disagree."

Someone yelled her name.

"I've got to go. I'm up next. It was nice to meet you."

He watched her walk off. "Amelia," he said, making her swing around to face him.

He smiled when a blush overtook her face as she looked around the room at the other girls, and her mouth dropped open.

"I just wanted to tell you it was nice to meet you."

She nodded, glanced at Price, and fled.

"Hey, um, mister."

Fury turned to see the woman who had sat with Amelia.

The woman looked back and forth between the men and swallowed hard.

"I ju … just wanted to tell you that Amelia is my friend and she's a very nice person. She's not going to w … w … want to be one of those girls in your club that…"

"Fuck every guy?" Fury asked helpfully and with a grin. She turned as red as Amelia had. It was something. For as long as he could remember, he'd never seen a stripper blush.

She cringed. "Yes. That. She's gone through so much. I don't want her hurt."

He was impressed. She was shaking, but she still stood up to him to protect her friend.

"She's a lot like Amelia, and both pretty much have the same story," Price told him.

"How about if I promise not to hurt her, and there's no way any other man will ever put his hands on her as long as she's with me? Will that help calm your fears?"

Tara nodded. "I guess that will have to do. I don't know what's happening or what you want from her, but I don't want you to keep us apart. We're best friends."

"I won't. I can see the two of you are close."

She nodded. "Okay. I've got to go. I'm up next."

He watched her scurry away, much like Amelia had.

"What do you think?" Price asked.

"I want her."

Price grinned. "I would worry if it were someone else, but I know you'll take care of her, and she needs that. She's been taking care of everyone else for so long."

"She'll be taken care of as long as she's with me."

"Can I give you a bit of advice?"

Fury nodded.

"Don't come on too strong, or she'll run."

"I gathered that," he said. "Let's go. I don't want to miss her set."

Fury sat as she was coming out on stage. The group of men roared their approval.

He'd tried to ignore the others and the streak of

jealousy he couldn't explain. He just wanted to watch.

A smile crossed his face when she glanced down at him and froze for a few seconds. The sound of the men seemed to bring her back, and she started to dance again.

"What's going on with her?" Traeger asked.

"I'm not sure yet, but I think I want her. Everything about her appeals to me."

"Do you think she could handle our way of life?"

"I think so. I'll have to be more protective, but I think the guys will take to her and help shield her."

Trager chuckled. "Oh, they're taking to her, but not the way you want them to. Every one of them has their tongues out and their eyes glued to her."

"Make sure you tell them hands-off."

"I will."

Amelia exited the stage, and Tara came on. She was a better dancer than Amelia, but he could tell she didn't like it any more than Amelia did.

"She's a hot little woman," Traeger murmured.

"She's Amelia's friend. They are a lot alike. If you want dibs on her, you better make it quick."

Traeger shrugged nonchalantly. "Maybe. I need to know more about her. I'll have Franky do a background check on both."

"Sounds good. I'm not a hundred percent sure about taking her on, but I think more information will help me decide."

"What's holding you back?"

Fury scowled. "My ex. She fucked me over so bad. I'm hesitant to try another relationship again."

"She was a skank."

Fury nodded. "Yeah, she was that."

"This one is pretty cute."

Fury nodded his agreement. He was itching to get the information on Amelia as quickly as possible, and then a thought crossed his mind.

He whistled to get Price's attention.

"Yeah, what's up, man?"

"How does she get home?"

"She drives here, and Tara takes the bus to come here, but after, Amelia drives her home."

"Anything I should worry about?"

"I don't know. Sorry. I tend to stay out of their personal lives as much as possible."

"Thanks. What car is Amelia's?"

"The blue four-door Ford in back."

"All right." Fury sat back and considered his options. He didn't like the thought of Amelia, hell, both of them out at night with no protection.

He knew right then he wasn't going to let them go off on their own. He just had to figure out a way to follow her and not terrify her.

Chapter Four

The dancers were still coming out when Fury stood.

"I'm leaving them in your hands, Traeger. I'm going to follow Amelia home to make sure she gets there safe."

Traeger grinned. "Already protective, I see."

"Yeah, I can't explain it, but I already feel like she's mine." Fury slapped him on the shoulder.

"Hey, Prez, are you headed home?" Enforcer asked.

"No. I'm going to check on something."

"Do you mind if I ride with you?"

"Sure, that's fine."

Fury got the time she got off work, and he was very close to having lost her.

He walked out of the strip joint, sat on his bike, and waited for Amelia's car to exit.

He knew Enforcer wanted to ask him questions, but he kept quiet, knowing he'd tell him eventually.

She pulled out of the back parking lot, turned, and drove past them. As far as he could tell, neither woman had noticed them sitting there on their bikes.

Enforcer shook his head in disgust. "Jesus, those women need a keeper."

Fury nodded and started his bike. He followed them at a discreet distance. They finally stopped at an apartment building, and Tara got out, turned, said something to Amelia, smiled, and shut the door.

He pulled over a block down and watched the woman make it to the building and go in. His attention returned to Amelia as she drove away.

The farther she drove into what he considered the

slum area of the city, the angrier he got. What the fuck was she doing coming down here by herself? It was like putting a kitten in with a lion.

Astonishment hit him when she pulled over at a decrepit, old apartment building. Cars on blocks, tall weeds, graffiti, garbage, and gang members were the scenery.

Anger raced through him when she got out and crossed the street. She didn't look around for any signs of danger and just walked along as calm as a nun in a church.

He'd shut off his bike as he watched her. His fingers went for the key when a few gang members walked up to her. At first, he thought they were harassing her, but she smiled, waved, and walked into the building.

"What the fuck?" Enforcer asked. "There are so many things wrong with this picture."

Fury nodded. "I agree."

He started his bike and pulled up to the group of young men. He turned his key, braced both legs out, and leaned forward with his forearms on his handlebars. "Hey."

They all turned his way. He was pleased to see the apprehension in every one of their eyes.

"What do you want?" one of them asked in a belligerent tone and stepped forward.

"I want to know about that woman you just talked to."

The guys looked at each other and then back at him.

"What about her?"

"Just tell me everything you know," Fury advised them and showing his impatience.

"Not much to tell. She's nice, keeps to herself for the most part, and hasn't lived here long."

Fury could tell they were leaving things out.

"Are you trying to protect her?" he asked the gang.

The front guy shrugged his shoulders. "She doesn't need to be hassled by guys like you."

He nodded. He was impressed they were standing up to him even though they were plainly nervous.

"I'm not used to explaining myself, but I can tell you I'm not here to hassle her. I've met Amelia, and she intrigues me. Then I find out where she lives, and it concerns me."

"We keep her safe."

"I'm sure you do, but can you tell me she's safe here all the time?"

The guys shook their heads.

"No, we've got some fuckheads who live around here that try to get to her, but we haven't let them."

"But you can't be here every minute she is. Right?"

The guy in front shook his head. "No, but she hasn't lived here too long, and she's not going to be here too much longer. After her dad died, she moved here to save money so she could move somewhere else."

Fury's eyes narrowed on the second-floor window, where he could see what he guessed was her shadow behind the curtain.

"I'm going to get her out of here."

"How do we know you're better for her?"

"You'll just have to take my word for it," Fury said. "If I were an asshole and wanted her, I'd just take her. Instead, I'm going to pay you guys to watch her every minute she's here until I can get her out."

"What if she doesn't want to go?" one of them asked.

Fury sighed. "That's why I'm doing it this way.

I'll let her get to know me better before I take her to my home. If she doesn't want that, I'll get her moved into another place that's safer."

The gang members nodded.

"We can do that. But you don't have to pay us. We were doing it already."

"I'm glad. I consider her mine, and I take care of what belongs to me. You'll still be paid."

"We'll do it, but if we find out you've hurt her, we'll be coming for you."

Fury and Enforcer chuckled. *Fuck, they are cute*, Fury thought. Little puppies trying to play at being men.

"Go ahead and chuckle, man. You might have a ton of bikers, but we have the advantage of being able to get close, and we'll blow you the fuck away."

Fury tipped his head forward. "Fair enough. I'll warn you that if anything happens to her before I can have her, I'll be coming after you, and I can guarantee I'm not going to need anyone else besides myself."

Fury watched to see if the guy understood. "Give me your number so I can check in with you. I'll also need a name and address to send the money to."

The first guy gave him the information, and then they walked toward the building. They all relaxed outside on the front steps. A few of them lit up a joint or cigarette.

Fury took another look at her window, turned his bike on, and rode out of the neighborhood.

He made a list in his head of the things he needed to do on the drive home. First and foremost, he needed to get her used to him and form a relationship, hopefully, the kind he wanted, but otherwise, he had a burning need to make sure she was safe.

Chapter Five

Amelia showed up for work the next day. She prayed on the way there. It was close to the last time she'd ever be able to say she was never going to strip again in a room full of perverts, but she knew it would take another few months to make enough to get her where she wanted to go.

She got out of her car in the back parking lot and stretched. She couldn't remember the last time she'd had a full night's sleep or felt rested. All she knew was that it was before her father got sick.

There wasn't a day that went by that she wasn't putting in at least ten hours of work. Besides Dick's Place, the strip joint she worked at, she put in several hours as a waitress at Fancy's Diner, and also stocked at a grocery store on the nights she wasn't stripping.

She figured the more she worked, the quicker she'd be able to leave.

"Hey, girl," Tara called from their small space in the corner they shared.

"Hi. You got here early."

"Mrs. Clark came early, so I took off."

Amelia sat down next to her and grabbed her hand. "Did she have another bad day?" she asked because of the stressed look on her friend's face.

Tara blinked back the tears that filled her eyes, making Amelia hurt for her.

"I'm moving her into the home I found sooner than I thought. She's deteriorating faster than the doctor predicted."

"Oh, God. That's awful. I'm so sorry."

Tara nodded.

Amelia wiped a tear from her cheek. "You'll be

able to see her any time, right?"

"They said if she had a good day that I could come see her, but if it's a bad day, it's better that I stay away because it might agitate her more."

Amelia's heart went out to her friend. "I'll do whatever you need."

Tara hugged her. "I know. You're the best friend I've ever had."

Both of them jerked apart when someone cleared their throat.

Amelia jumped up to face the man from the night before. He was scary as hell but also incredibly compelling and attractive. His body was huge and very muscular with tattoos down his arms, and she caught sight of the tip of one above his black t-shirt that molded to his body.

His blue jeans were tight and showed how thick his thighs were. He wore boots that made him even taller and a vest with patches.

She waited for him to say something, and when he just stared, she started to get more anxious. She stepped in front of Tara, hoping to protect her from the unseen threat.

Amelia cleared her throat. "Um … you're not supposed to be back here."

He smirked and crossed his arms over his chest.

Amelia looked around for Price, and then her gaze landed on the man again. "What can I do for you? I don't have time to play the staring game."

Tara gasped behind her, and the guy's eyebrows rose in surprise.

She had to take her attention off him when Tara tried to get in front of her, but there wasn't a lot of space in the corner, so the wall and the table kept Tara behind Amelia.

"Stop it, Tara."

"No, you stop it. Are you crazy? You can't talk like that to him," Tara hissed.

Amelia turned to face her. "Why not? He started it," she complained.

****

Fury had to bite his lip to keep from laughing as the two girls fought over who was going to protect who against him. He sighed and leaned back against the wall, and waited.

"What's going on?"

Fury looked at Traeger over his shoulder.

"They're trying to figure out who will protect who against mean old me."

Traeger barked out a laugh, catching the girls' attention.

"Have you decided?" Fury asked in a calm tone.

"Decided what?" Amelia asked with a scowl.

"Who's going to deal with me."

She narrowed her eyes. "Who are you here to see?"

"You."

"Ha," Amelia said after she turned back to Tara.

"That doesn't mean I will let you get hurt because I won't," Tara almost yelled.

They started yelling at each other again.

"Is that the one you were telling me about?"

Fury nodded at Traeger's question. "Price told me they are BFFs," he said and smirked.

"She's a cutie except for the ugly wig she has on."

Fury nodded. "I don't like Amelia's either. They wear them here so people they know don't see them."

Traeger chuckled. "I wonder if that works."

Fury grunted.

"Amelia, you're up in five," someone yelled.

They stopped yelling at each other.

She turned to him. Her eyes widened when she caught sight of Traeger.

"How many of you are there?"

Fury shook his head, and Traeger laughed.

"A lot. Shouldn't you be getting ready?"

She gasped. "But you're still standing here. You have to go."

Fury rolled his eyes. "Babe, you're going to be showing a lot of men your body shortly." He swallowed back the rage he felt at the thought of so many men seeing her nearly naked.

"That's different. I have to take off my bra and panties and then put on the costume."

He tilted his head forward. "All right, go ahead."

"I'm not doing it in front of you," she bellowed.

His eyebrows went up.

Traeger snorted behind him. "When's the last time someone has yelled at you or a woman you want to get naked fights you?"

"Decades," he murmured to his friend without taking his gaze off of Amelia. He should be pissed, but it just made him want her more.

"I'm not leaving."

She stomped her foot. "Yes, you are."

He rolled his eyes and straightened. "If you want, I can help you," he murmured menacingly with a raised brow.

Both girls whispered frantically to each other before Tara stood in front of Amelia and blocked his view as she changed into her costume. Then, Amelia did the same for Tara until they both stood in front of him and smiled in satisfaction.

Traeger started laughing hysterically.

Fury walked up to Amelia and cupped her cheek.

"That was very inventive, babe."

"Thank you."

He pressed a hard kiss to her lips and then smiled when she gasped and tried to take a step away, but he just pinched her chin. "I'll be out in front."

"Why did you have to tell me that?" she asked, disgruntled.

He smirked and shrugged.

She hissed and tried to slap his hand away.

He shook his head and yanked her into his arms, and dropped his mouth to take hers. His tongue dived into the depths of hers, tasting her and stroking. A short moment later, he lifted his head and was extremely pleased when she stood still, her eyes mostly closed with a dazed look in them. Her lips were swollen and red.

He turned her when he heard someone call for her. "Go dance. We'll talk later."

A chuckle burst from his lips when she about ran into the wall. Fuck, he loved that he could do that to her.

"I'm going back out front," he told Tara. "By the way, this is Traeger."

He watched Tara fidget, unable to take her eyes off his friend, and a smile formed across Traeger's face.

He rolled his eyes. He'd let them deal with it. His woman was out front, and he wasn't going to miss her dance.

Chapter Six

Bull handed him a beer when he sat down just as Amelia walked out on the stage. He leaned back and straightened his legs under the table. As he sipped his beer, he never took his eyes off her.

He was extremely pleased when she caught sight of him, blushed scarlet, froze, and stared at him like she had the night before.

Someone yelled at her to get her to start dancing, and she jerked and turned away. She seemed to try really hard not to look his way, but he saw her trying to catch a glimpse of him several times.

Finally, her set was done, and he could relax, but Price had told him she had three routines tonight, so he had two more to go. He'd have to deal with men looking at her a few more times that night.

He was impressed with Tara's dancing, although he could tell she didn't enjoy it. He grinned at the look on Traeger's face. He had guessed before they had ever met that his friend would be attracted to her. They had both talked about the woman they wanted to find for themselves because they hated sharing the whores with the rest of the club.

He actually hadn't fucked anyone in longer than he'd ever admit to anyone.

A commotion behind the stage caught his attention. He stood when he heard Amelia's voice and saw Tara stop dancing and rush back.

"I'm going to check this out."

He walked in and saw one of the other strippers, Amelia, and Price, in a circle yelling at each other.

Tara stepped off the stage and joined them. Pretty soon, she was yelling as well.

"She did not, you skanky bitch," Tara yelled.

He finally whistled to get everyone to shut up.

He looked at Price. "What's going on?"

Price sighed. "Sadie is accusing Amelia of stealing some money from her."

Fury glanced at Amelia. There was not an ounce of guilt on her face. The only emotions he saw were embarrassment and sorrow. He knew the slut was lying.

"When do you think she did it?" he asked Sadie.

"Right after she got here. She's a liar and a thief," Sadie shrieked. "You don't want to be with a slut you can't trust."

His brows snapped together. "For one thing, don't ever call Amelia a slut, or I'll cut out your tongue," he said. "Secondly, I was back here from the time she got here until she went on stage, so she had no time."

"I don't believe that."

He pulled himself back from smacking the bitch and instead turned to Price. "Why don't we just look at the footage of the last hour?"

"Footage of what?" Sadie asked suspiciously.

"The owner has hidden cameras everywhere."

All three women gasped in shock and started looking around the room for the cameras. Price looked over their shoulders and grinned at him.

Fury had lied about the cameras because he thought it would be a quick answer to who was telling the truth even though everyone knew which one was lying.

Fury cleared his throat to get their attention.

"So, Sadie, we can find out within the hour what happened, and if we find you were lying about Amelia stealing from you, you not only will be fired, but I'm also going to hurt you for upsetting her."

Sadie's mouth opened and closed a few times.

"Answer me," Fury barked.

"Fuck, fine. She didn't do anything."

"Then why pull this shit?" Price asked angrily.

"Because I'm sick of her and Tara getting all the attention. The only strippers the guys want to meet are those two fat bitches, and I'm sick of it."

Fury stepped forward and grasped Sadie's upper arm before looking at Tara and Amelia.

His expression and tone gentled. "Why don't you girls head back to your table and get ready for your next set, and Price can go up front while this bitch and I have a little talk."

Amelia and Tara walked off but kept on looking back. He waited until they turned the corner to step into their own dressing area before he yanked Sadie up close and bent over.

"I'm only going to warn you once that if you ever mess with either of those women again, they won't be able to find your body."

She tried to jerk away from him. "You're full of shit," she hissed.

He smiled, but he knew it wasn't a friendly smile but the vicious one, and was pleased when she seemed to realize how much danger she was really in.

"I'm the prez of the Devil's Sons, you stupid cunt. Do you really think I give two shits about your skanky ass? You think that I can't make you disappear?"

She swallowed and slowly shook her head.

"Just so we understand each other. You fuck with what's mine, and you die. It's simple."

"Fuck, fine," she cried. "Now, let me go."

He pushed her away from him and watched her walk away before strolling back to the girls' area to find Amelia crying and Tara hugging her.

He sighed and tapped Tara on the shoulder. "Let me take her while you go do your set."

Tara looked back and forth and only left when Amelia nodded. "Fine, but I'll be right back."

He didn't wait but pulled Amelia into his arms. She stiffened for a moment and pushed at his stomach, then quickly gave up before wrapping her arms around his waist and started crying again.

"Shh, babe. Everything is good. You never have to worry about her again." He reached for a few tissues when she started to settle down. "Here, wipe your tears and blow your nose."

She tried to step back to get a little bit of room between them. Then she huffed and wrestled her arms enough to be able to reach her face. "You could make this a bit easier," she grumbled.

He chuckled. "Naw, I'm good." He laughed when she growled and hit his side with her tiny fist. He grunted for her benefit but hadn't really felt anything. His sneezes had more sensation than her abuse.

He tipped her head back with his fingers under her chin.

"Does it look like I've been crying?" she asked and sniffed.

He had to bite his lip to keep from laughing because her eyes were red and swollen, and her makeup was in streaks down her splotchy face.

"No, not really. Give me a Kleenex, and I'll help."

She tipped her face up for him so he could start wiping the makeup away, and he found it utterly adorable. He tried to remember when or if he'd ever helped a woman do this, but he hadn't cared enough for anyone. Not even his ex, Dana.

He was the prez of the most feared MC around, and here he was, helping with makeup.

"Is it off?"

He nodded. "Yes."

She turned, bent to look in the mirror, and then gasped. "I look horrible. Oh, my God. I go on in a few minutes."

She sat on one of the stools and started caking on the makeup.

"I hate that shit. I don't like you wearing it."

She looked at his reflection in the mirror. "I have to wear it, and besides, you can't tell me what I can and can't do."

Fury leaned back against the wall and crossed his arms before he smirked at her. "We'll have to see about that."

Amelia snorted and finished her makeup right as someone called for her. She stood and turned and looked at his chest.

"Oh, I'm sorry, I got your shirt all wet."

He grunted. "Honey, that's not the only thing you got wet."

She looked up at him in confusion.

He rolled his eyes. "Never mind. You better go."

She took a few steps away from him before he jerked her back into his arms, lowered his head, and took her lips possessively and with a hunger that surprised even him.

"There. I feel better," he murmured against her lips before he released her.

When she scowled at him before she turned the corner, he grinned. He wanted her more and more every day. He just needed her to trust him before they moved on.

He watched her when she came back to fix her makeup for her last dance. It was hilarious that she tried to ignore him.

"I want to take you out after this."

She shook her head. "No."

He grinned and shook his head in confusion. No one ever told him no. "How about just for coffee?"

"No." She stood up and smoothed out her outfit.

"I'll just keep coming back here."

"And I'll keep ignoring you," she told him smugly.

He smirked and yanked her into his arms. Then he took her mouth in a kiss that left him breathless and achy.

"That right there tells you how good we'll be together." He watched her gather her wits before she scowled up at him.

"You have to stop doing that."

He shook his head. "No. Doesn't that sound familiar?"

She growled and hit his side again.

"I'll just keep trying."

"And I'll keep saying no."

"We'll see, babe."

She started to walk away. "We sure will, babe."

He grinned when she scurried away from him. Oh, he'd eventually get her precisely the way he wanted her, in his home and under him.

Chapter Seven

One particular night, Fury followed her home, like he had every night after she worked at the club for the last few weeks. Every time he saw where she lived, he became angrier.

It helped that the guys he paid to watch over her were there every time.

He waited until she went into her apartment building before he pulled up to the gang.

The leader, who he found out went by Skid, walked up to him.

"How's everything going?" Fury asked after he shut off the motorcycle.

"Good. Some punk tried to hassle her after she got home from one of her other jobs…"

Fury's brows snapped together. "Wait. What other jobs? I thought she only worked at the strip joint."

"She works at Fancy's Diner every day, and at night, she stocks shelves at Mercer Grocery on the days she doesn't work at the club."

Fury's jaw throbbed as anger raced through him. How in the fuck did he miss that? "What the fuck?"

"Yeah, it's bullshit. She comes home most nights beyond exhausted."

Fury wiped a hand down his face.

"Hey!"

Fury and Skid turned toward the building to see Amelia leaning out the window and scowling at them.

Fury grinned. "Hey, what?" he yelled back.

"What the hell are you doing here, Fury?"

He chuckled at the look of shock on the guys' faces.

"I'm checking on my woman."

They all heard her growl, and then the window slammed down. He was surprised it hadn't shattered.

He got off his bike when she came storming out of the building in nothing but a robe and little bunny slippers.

"I'm not kidding, Fury. I want to know why you're here. Are you following me?"

He was pissed at her lack of fear. They were in one of the worst neighborhoods in the city with a gang of thugs and an MC Prez outside, and she ran out looking like that.

He glanced at Skid. "I'm taking her back in. I need you to watch my bike."

"You got it," Skid said and laughed when Fury walked toward her, picked her up, and tossed her over his shoulder, never breaking stride.

Fury let her smack his back and scream out her anger as he walked up the stairs and then into her apartment.

He set her down, locked the door, and then turned to confront her. His eyes widened when he saw her with her arms crossed angrily over her chest and one of her feet tapping.

The fact the foot in question had a fluffy bunny slipper on it and the ears of the thing flopped around with her movements, as cute as it was, made it hard to take her seriously, and it didn't deflect from his anger over her working so many jobs and then coming outside in the robe she had on.

"What the hell do you think you're doing, woman?" he bellowed.

He didn't think he raised his voice until he heard it bounce off the walls inside the apartment and saw her take a step back.

"Oh, no, woman. You will not fear me. Do you

understand?"

Her chin went up. "I'm not afraid. I just don't like to be yelled at."

He exhaled and set his hands on his hips. His gaze started at the bunnies and moved up over her luscious curves. In the strip club, she showed more skin, but for some reason, standing in her robe made her look even sexier. His palms itched to touch her.

"Tell me why in the hell you have three jobs."

She looked confused. "So I can save money faster."

"For what?"

"I'm planning on moving."

The thought of never seeing her again made him almost sick.

"Where?"

"I'm not sure yet."

His shock must have been apparent because her back stiffened and her eyes narrowed. "I keep looking at a map, but nothing ever pops out at me. I thought about throwing a dart, but I haven't found one yet," she said defensively.

Fury shook his head, surprised, and tried to hide his smile. Could she get any cuter?

He walked over to the window and looked out at the gang as they stood in front of his bike, but he wasn't really seeing them. He concentrated on coming up with a solution for keeping her in the city.

He wanted to demand she come home with him, where he'd been trying to get her, but she had an independent streak a mile wide, and he didn't want her to build a wall between them or run.

Fury saw he startled her when he spun around.

"Can you cook?"

"Well, yes. Why?"

"We need someone to cook for us."

She looked at him suspiciously. "I don't think you're telling me the truth."

He walked to her and cupped her chin. "I swear to you that I'm not lying."

His mind tried to come up with anything that might persuade her. "We need you, babe."

Her eyes widened. "You need me? Really?"

"Yes. We have two guys who can cook, but they're not great at it. We usually call out for pizza or burgers."

"Are you trying to kill yourself?" she snapped and scowled.

He grinned. "No. But if we keep going the way we are, we'll probably all have heart attacks."

He could tell he was getting her attention. He was laying it on thick, but he now knew the way to get to her. Through sympathy, using guilt, and needing her.

"Let me think about it."

He nodded. "All right. You have two minutes."

She snorted and rolled her eyes but then started pacing in front of him, pulling at her bottom lip with her fingers and staring at the floor while she debated.

She stopped in front of him. "That's all I'd do, right? Just cook. I wouldn't have to … you know, the guys?"

"I can guarantee no one will touch you except me."

"What if I don't want you to touch me?"

"If you can kiss me without becoming aroused, I'll leave you alone."

She held a hand out when he stepped toward her. "Whoa. We've already kissed several times, and we both know I like it, so you don't have to do it now. It will just muddle my brain."

"Fine. Have you decided?"

"No, not yet." She started pacing again.

Fury sighed and had to fight not to grab her as she passed him. He thought about all the things he wanted to do to her when he got her back to the clubhouse, but he wouldn't do it until she was ready, but he'd make sure that didn't take long.

He was pulled from his thoughts when she stopped in front of him again.

"What about Tara?"

His brows drew together. "What about her?"

"She has to come work with me."

"Hell," he growled. "Fine, she can come too, but we're all going to have to go over some things and come to an understanding. Okay? So, you're saying you'll come with me?"

She nodded. "If you tell me what times you think I can come to work but maybe keep one of my other jobs."

He looked up to the ceiling. "Babe, you won't be working anywhere else. Neither of you will, and you'll both move into the clubhouse with us."

"Wait, we have to live with you?" she asked with wide eyes.

"Yes. That's non-negotiable."

"Oh, I don't know…"

He grasped her shoulders and bent so he could see her clearly and look her straight in the eye.

She must have detected his determination because she sighed.

"Okay, fine. We can do that. But I get my own bedroom, right?"

Fuck. He wanted to yell *no* but knew he was pushing her already, and she looked ready to drop.

"Yes, for the time being. Your job will be to take

care of us, and in return, you'll get paid, but you'll also have our protection."

"I'm not sure…"

"We need you, babe."

It was underhanded to use her caring nature, but he was desperate to get her to the club where he could watch over her. The fact she hadn't already gotten hurt made him anxious at the thought of protecting her. Surely her luck would give out soon.

"You really need me?"

"Yes. You'll see I'm not lying when we're there."

She exhaled and smiled. "Okay, I'll give my two weeks, not…"

"No. I'll call your bosses, and you're moving tonight."

"What? Wait. I've got so much to pack."

"I'll call the guys, and they'll bring a few trucks. With their help, we can have you back at the clubhouse within a few hours."

"And we can't wait until tomorrow?"

He shook his head.

She ran her fingers through her hair. "It's so sudden, and I'm already tired. I don't know."

"You won't have to do anything. Please." Fuck, when was the last time he said that word? "I won't be able to sleep tonight if you're not in the club."

She studied his face for a long moment and then nodded. "Okay, I'll get dressed."

"You do that, and I'll call my guys."

He watched her walk away and tried to hide his elation long enough for her to disappear into her bedroom, so she didn't see it. He pulled his phone out and called Traeger. He explained what was going on and ignored his laughter.

"Just get your fucking ass here, pronto."

"We're on our way."

He walked into her bedroom to see she had dressed in jeans that showed her curves and a loose green striped t-shirt. She was putting things in several bags she had sitting on her bed.

"Hey, babe, what can I help with?"

She looked around. "Nothing right now. I don't have a lot of clothes."

"What about the furniture and stuff in the kitchen?"

"None of the furniture is mine, but everything else is. We can use some boxes I've been hoarding for when I move. There are flat and under the bed. The tape is in the kitchen."

"I'll start in the kitchen while you work in here."

She nodded and went back to packing.

He knew he probably wasn't doing it right, but he threw things into a few boxes. His primary and only objective was to get her home where she belonged.

Chapter Eight

Amelia had everything out of her closet and drawers on her bed, so she folded them and put them into a box Fury had brought her.

It startled her when someone banged against her door with what she guessed was a fist. She raced out of the bedroom and came to a screeching stop when twelve to fifteen huge guys walked into her apartment, turned, and stared at her.

"Men, this is Amelia, and she's mine. Everything but the furniture goes. When a box is full, take it out to the trucks. We should be able to get everything packed up quickly. Be careful with everything."

"You got it, boss," several of them said and got to work.

She was stunned when all the men started grabbing things and either putting them in a box or taking them out to the truck.

A few of the guys walked past her into the bedroom and started putting clothes in a box. She blushed scarlet red when one of them lifted a pair of her panties and grinned at the other guy.

She raced to them and snatched her underwear from his fingers.

"No touching the undies," she said with a growl.

Both looked shocked, but then one of them scowled down at her, which pissed her off, so she lifted her chin and scowled right back at him.

His eyebrows rose while the other guy chuckled.

"Do you understand, buddy?" She pointed a finger at him.

He raised both hands and took a step back.

"Yeah, I got it."

Amelia shoved the last of her clothes and shoes in

the bags and box and dumped the things in the bathroom in a box one of the guys gave her.

Within twenty minutes, they were done, and the truck and the guys were gone.

She stood in the middle of the living room and turned around, taking everything in. The place was bare and silent, and she felt a bit sad that she was leaving the only place she'd called her own. Her whole life, she'd lived at home, and the last couple of years, she'd taken care of her father, so she'd never had her own place that she never had to share.

It hadn't made her as happy as she thought it would. Instead of feeling free, she felt isolated and lonely, and sometimes a little scared.

A smile crossed her face. She'd never be lonely again, living with a bunch of guys and Tara.

She was startled when arms came around her middle from behind. Right off the bat, she knew who it was by his masculine scent.

"Are you okay?"

She nodded. "Yeah. It just feels weird."

"I'll do whatever I can to make you happy, so you'll want to stay with us and with me."

"I have to call Tara."

He nodded. "Let's get you back to the club, and you can call her in the morning. It's really late."

"Okay. I'm ready."

She grabbed the hand he held out to her and let him pull her along. Out on the sidewalk, the guys she'd met right after she'd moved in were in a group.

She walked up to Skid and hugged him. "Thank you for making me feel safe."

Skid had stiffened but relaxed when he looked at Fury and then wrapped her in his arms.

"You're welcome, *chica*. You stay safe."

"You too." She waved at the group, walked to Fury, and retook his hand.

"Did one of my guys take care of you?" Fury asked Skid.

"Yeah, man. Thanks."

"I owe you, so if you ever need something, call the clubhouse."

"You got it."

Amelia ignored them and stopped abruptly at the end of the sidewalk.

"Wait, where's my car?"

"One of the guys took that, and another took my bike. I wanted to drive you."

"Oh." That was all she could think of to say. She could feel her energy level drop by the second.

"Come on, let's get you home."

On the way back to the clubhouse, Amelia's thoughts became more jumbled. She couldn't concentrate on just one thing.

"Just relax, babe. We'll be home shortly."

She nodded, laid her head against the window, and closed her eyes.

The next thing she knew, they were parked behind a huge building, and Fury was unbuckling her seatbelt.

"I'm sorry. I didn't mean to go to sleep."

"I wanted you to rest. You're exhausted."

He picked her up in his arms.

"Wait," she screeched. "I can walk."

He shook his head. "I've got you, so just relax."

She put her arms around his neck and laid against his chest.

They walked through a vast room, ignoring the people sitting or standing around, and up a flight of stairs.

"I'm putting you in here. It will eventually be Traeger's room, but he hasn't had time to move his shit from his other room."

"What happens when he's ready?"

"We'll figure it out when we have to."

He set her down and let her look around. The room was immense. There was a huge bed and a dresser, an entertainment center with a large TV. She saw the walk-in closet had more than enough space, and the bathroom was luxurious.

"This all looks new," she said and turned back to him.

"It is. We added the addition this summer. The club is growing, and the building we added on to was too small. We'll still use the bedrooms and everything else, but we're getting used to this side of the building. We also put in a huge kitchen. I'll show you tomorrow."

"Okay. Am I only staying in here tonight?"

"I think we'll put you and Tara together until we figure things out. Do you guys think you can share?"

"Of course."

****

Fury grinned when she sat down wearily on the edge of the mattress. There wasn't even a sheet on the new bed, but he figured he'd get her a pillow and blanket, and he'd deal with the rest tomorrow.

He walked out, and when he came back, she was on her back with her legs over the edge of the mattress, passed out. He chuckled before he pulled off her shoes, socks, and jeans, trying to ignore the white panties and short t-shirt she wore. After wrapping the blanket around her, he lifted her and placed her head on the pillow.

He chuckled a few times when she grumbled something but never awoke.

At the door, he turned back before flicking off the light. It took every bit of strength he had to shut the door and walk away. He kept telling himself he'd have her sooner rather than later. He was surprised at how patient he'd been with her. Before her, if he wanted something, he usually just took it. Instead, he'd been watching her strip every Friday and Saturday night for the last few weeks and only getting to talk to her when she was there.

He'd always thought she looked tired, and now he knew why. Fuck, he couldn't believe he'd just found out she was working three jobs. That could have been the reason she'd turned him down when he wanted to spend time with her.

Now that he had her in his own space, he'd be able to get at her all the fucking time.

He walked back downstairs and saw all her things stacked in one corner.

"Hey, can you and a few guys take all this up to my room? I'll have her deal with it tomorrow."

Several men grabbed a bunch of things, so they'd only have to make one trip.

Fury walked through the building, making sure everything was okay. He found a few of the guys fucking the club whores and some in a game of poker he hoped didn't get out of hand because a few of them liked to cheat.

He finally found Traeger working on his bike in the vast warehouse-sized building they used for their boy toys, like the motorcycles, souped-up cars, and four-wheelers.

"Is she settled?"

Fury leaned against the tool bench, crossed his arms over his chest, and nodded. "Yeah, she's out."

"Hopefully, she won't wake up and freak because she doesn't know where she is."

"I'm planning on going up and leaving my door open."

"You're not going to crash with her?" Trager said

and grinned.

"As much as I want to, I don't want to fuck this up."

Traeger nodded as he polished the chrome on his bike.

"When are you planning on moving into your room?"

"It doesn't matter to me. If she needs it, let her have it."

"It shouldn't be too long."

"You hope." Traeger chuckled.

"Fuck off. I'm also putting Tara in there. They'll share until we figure things out."

Fury watched his friend turn away.

"Are you pissed that she's coming too?"

"No. Not at all," Traeger answered.

Fury narrowed his eyes at the tone of Traeger's voice. "What do you want me to tell the guys? Is she up for grabs?"

"Sure. I'm not ready for a full-time woman."

Fury growled. "Jesus, it wasn't your fucking fault. When are you going to get over it?"

Traeger stood and faced him. At first, Fury thought his friend would hit him with the silver ratchet in his grip. He waited, tense and ready.

"Just fucking shut up about it," Traeger said and walked away.

"Fine, you stupid fuck. The guys will be thrilled at a chance at her."

Fury rolled his eyes when Traeger ignored him and began to organize the tools on the far bench.

He turned and walked into the back door to the kitchen. The place was a mess again, which pissed him off. Then he went into the large living area. It had a big TV room that opened up into a game room and enough space for anything else. When they'd made the add-on plans, he'd made sure he got everything he thought his guys would need.

"Some of you guys and whores not doing anything, get in the kitchen and clean it up. It looks like shit again. If you can't pick up after yourselves, I'll put you back in the old place, and you can just stay in that."

"We'll get it done, boss."

"You better. And before tomorrow morning." He walked up the stairs and down the hall. He cracked open Amelia's door to check on her. She was on her stomach in the middle of the mattress with the blanket pushed down to the end of the bed, and her shirt had pulled up, leaving her lower part of her body in nothing besides panties.

He cursed as a drop of sweat ran down the side of his face. Jesus, he wouldn't be able to deal with having her around and not being able to touch her for long.

He held his breath when she turned on her side and sighed his name.

He thought she saw him at first, but her eyes were still closed, and her breathing was deep and even.

It gave him hope that she was dreaming about him.

He'd see how she acted in the morning. At that moment, he needed to get some sleep. He just wished it could be beside her.

Chapter Nine

Amelia squinted her eyes against the sunlight seeping in through the window. She sat up and looked around the room. It took her a minute to remember where she was before she looked around for her clothes, which she found folded on the dresser.

She couldn't remember taking them off the night before, which bothered her, but she snatched them up and went into the bathroom. Someone, most likely Fury, had put her things in the room for her. After a quick shower and brushing her teeth, she brushed her hair with her fingers and left the room.

She couldn't remember which way to go until she heard several voices down the hall. Her grip on the stair railing tightened as more guys stopped talking and turned to stare at her.

She stopped at the bottom step and waited. Surprise crossed her face when she heard Tara. Forgetting about the men, she hurried toward where the sound was coming from.

When she burst into the kitchen, she saw Tara at the stove, stirring something in a big pan and a few of the men she didn't know talking to her.

Amelia smiled when she finally got her attention. Tara burst out a laugh and ran to her. They hugged for a long time until they both smelled something burning and raced to the stove.

Fortunately, the eggs were saved. Amelia was shocked at the size of the pan.

"How many eggs do you have in that pan?"

Tara chuckled. "Four dozen."

"Well, I would say that's too much, but with the group of men here and all of them oversized, we might just run out. What can I do while we talk?"

"Toast. There are two large warmers next to the stove. You can put them in when you're done with a group."

Amelia looked around the room in awe. She'd never seen a kitchen this large or equipped with everything they would need except in restaurants.

The enormous refrigerator was industrial size, and it didn't have a freezer, so she assumed it was somewhere else.

"So, tell me how you got here. I was planning on calling you this morning and asking you if you'd like to stay here with me."

Tara snorted. "I certainly wasn't asked in a normal way." She dumped the eggs in a large glass bowl and set it in one of the warmers before she started on the bacon. "There was a knock on my door about six this morning. I recognized Fury's voice from Dick's Place, so I opened it."

"Oh, Lord. What happened?"

"He stepped into my apartment and told me you were living and working here and wanted me to come with you. I asked a bunch of questions before I finally agreed. Not two minutes after that, several men walked into my place and started packing everything. They had to have been waiting outside for the go-ahead. That told me I probably didn't have a choice about moving, but thankfully, I wanted to. I just stood there with my mouth open until Fury barked at me to tell them what was going. By eight, I was packed up, here, and starting breakfast."

Amelia laughed, which brought more men into the kitchen. Before the women knew it, twelve guys stood there watching them.

"Hey, guys, it's not quite done. We can yell when it is," Amelia told them as she buttered more toast.

"That's okay. We'll wait."

Amelia turned back to the toast and rolled her eyes.

Both women jumped when someone yelled from the door to go outside.

"What the fuck are you guys doing?"

"We're just watching, boss."

Amelia's heartbeat rose, and she could feel a flush cover her face when Fury looked at her.

He sighed. "Do you guys mind if you're gawked at?"

She and Tara shrugged.

"Not as long as they stay out of the way," Amelia said.

She went back to the toast and tried to calm her breathing but gasped when a hot, hard body pressed against her back, and his two hands gripped her hips.

"Good morning."

A shiver raced through her at his low, masculine tone, making him chuckle. Her blush deepened because he knew what caused it.

"Um … good morning."

"Did you sleep good, babe?"

"Ah, no … I mean, yeah."

He pressed the ridge of his cock against the crease of her ass. "Didn't I tell you we needed you?"

She nodded.

He grinned. "I'll leave you to it. If the guys get obnoxious, throw something at them."

"We will," she called out to him before he walked out the door. "Thank you for bringing Tara here."

"You can thank me later." He turned and left.

She frowned at the doorway. "What does that mean?" Her gaze jumped to the guys when they laughed.

"Bacon is about done."

Amelia finished toasting two loaves of bread and helped Tara pour glasses of orange juice, coffee, and milk. They set everything out on the island counter for the guys to feed themselves.

The women watched in amazement as the food dwindled rather quickly, but at least they thought most all of them had gone through.

"We better scramble some more eggs," Amelia said and started cracking them into a bowl while Tara heated the pan. Within a few minutes, they filled the bowl with eggs and started on some more toast.

The women leaned against the counter, drank coffee, and watched the men when Fury and Traeger came into the kitchen.

Amelia's heartbeat instantly rose.

Fortunately, there was some food left, and she and Tara made two plates for the guys while they filled their cups with coffee.

"Here you go," she told Fury. "Tara and I will figure out how much you all eat."

Fury snorted. "It wouldn't matter. They keep eating until it's gone. Just do the best you can, and it's a hell of a lot more than they were getting."

She nodded and watched as they walked out of the room, talking with their plates in their hands. The girls grabbed the bowls and put them to soak in the sink as they wiped up the kitchen.

"Hey, my mom was taken to the home that specializes in her condition in an ambulance last night. She'd gotten out of the house and was walking around outside."

Amelia pressed a hand to her mouth. She thought her mother was already in the home because Tara talked about it. "Oh, my God. Is she okay?"

"Yes."

"You sounded like she was already there."

"I'm sorry. I don't like to talk about it."

"I understand that," Amelia said and hugged her. "I'm so sorry."

Tara wiped a tear from her eye. "I hate to say that I'm glad it happened."

"I understand. You kept her with you longer than most everyone would have."

"Am I always going to feel like it wasn't enough?"

"Yeah. But it gets easier."

They made themselves a few eggs and toast and stood at the long island, eating while they made a list of the different things they could make for the meals.

Amelia's head jerked up as five scantily clad women stumbled into the kitchen. They looked rough, like they had just woken up from being brutally used the night before.

"Where the fuck is the food?" one of them yelled as they looked around.

Amelia and Tara glanced at each other, not knowing what to do.

Amelia cleared her throat. "I'm sorry, but it's gone."

"Then make us some more," a thin fake redhead said.

"That's not going to fucking happen."

All the women turned toward the door.

"If you whores can't get up at a reasonable time, you feed yourselves, and you better damn well clean up after yourselves, or you're banned from the kitchen."

Amelia bit her lip as she watched Traeger. He set two plates and cups in the sink.

"That's not fucking fair."

Amelia and Tara glanced at each other as Traeger

stalked toward the woman.

Amelia gasped when he took a chuck of the mouthy one's hair and got in her face.

"You don't fucking get it, whore. You're here for one reason, and that's a hole for the boys to fuck. Maybe if you'd get off your scrawny ass and help around here, I'd go easier on you, but all you do is sit around or fuck. No one would think twice about you if you disappeared, so watch yourself."

He yanked her head away from him, making her cry out in pain, and walked out.

Amelia and Tara didn't know what to do.

"You fucking skanks, you're here to be maids and nothing else. So stay the fuck away from the guys."

The group turned and walked out.

Amelia exhaled and grabbed Tara's hand. "That was intense."

Tara laughed. "Ya think?"

"Let's go back to the list of meals, and then I think we should set up a menu plan for the whole week then make a grocery list. What do you think?"

Tara nodded. "I think that's the most efficient way we can do it. We also need to go through the pantry, refrigerator, and freezer to see what's available. We could make an inventory of it to help us keep track."

"Great idea. I think we should try to make the food they have here already."

A few hours later, both women were wiping the sweat off their faces as they cleaned, inventoried, and organized the pantry. They hadn't even gotten to the cold items yet.

"God, I'm glad Fury let you come with me. I could never have done this by myself very easily."

Tara chuckled. "I'm glad too. Although I never saw myself living with a motorcycle gang, you're the only person in my life I care about besides my mom, so the thought of living and working with you was great."

Amelia handed her a glass of lemonade. "You're like the sister I always dreamed of."

"Ditto," Tara said and fist-bumped her.

Amelia looked at the clock. "Hell, we better get lunch going."

She and Tara started pulling out the sandwich meats and setting that, bread, and the condiments on the long island they were using as a buffet. It made it easier to serve on one side and have the guys go in a line on the other.

They pulled out pickles and whatever chips they could find.

"This is the best we can do, I guess."

Tara nodded. "I think they'll be pleased with this. We could make some soups and chili a few times a week too."

"I think we put that on our list."

She had just set paper plates and napkins down when the women came in. Without a word, they grabbed a bunch of the food, filling their plates to the brim.

Amelia glanced at Tara. She hoped they had enough for everybody because if these tiny women ate like this, the men would be a lot worse.

A few of the girls gave them a smug smile and walked out to the backyard.

A stream of guys came through at a steady pace.

"I think we should make Fury and Traeger a plate again before it's all gone."

Tara nodded, and they made up two large sandwiches and chips on each plate, covered them, and set them aside.

"While the club is getting their food, let's start on dinner."

Tara nodded. "We have the fixings for chili and cornbread."

"Let's do that. Have you been through the spices?"

"Yeah," Tara said as she started to pull the ones she needed out. "But we need to make a list of the ones we'll need."

Amelia went over the spices. "The chili won't be award-winning, but it will taste good enough. Especially with what we have to work with."

"I think the guys will be happy with whatever we make."

"From what I understand, they'll be happy no matter what." Amelia grinned.

Chapter Ten

"Hey, babe," someone said behind them, but they ignored it because they thought they were talking to someone else.

Traeger snorted. "I don't think she knows you're talking to her."

Fury grunted, walked over to Amelia, and placed a hand on her lower back, which startled her.

Her body jerked before she turned toward him. "Oh, hey, sorry. What do you need?"

He looked her over and didn't like the flush and the film of sweat on the women's faces.

"I didn't know this would be so hard, babe."

"But it's not. Tara and I are doing inventory and organizing. When that's done, it will go much smoother."

He smoothed the hair from her face. "I don't want you overdoing it."

She snorted. "This is a breeze compared to what I was doing for the last several weeks."

He didn't like hearing about what she'd been through lately, but now that he was in her life, he'd do what he could to make life easier for her.

Fury watched Traeger talk to Tara. He could see the attraction between the two but knew Traeger was still dealing with his girlfriend's death that he felt responsible for. He hoped his friend gave the woman a chance. She seemed to be as sweet as Amelia.

The back door slammed, catching his attention. The whores that walked in froze at the sight of the prez and vice-prez.

He looked at the massive amount of food still on their plates and then at them. "You're eating all of that. If you put it on your plate, it won't go to waste. Enforcer!"

Fury yelled.

"Yeah, boss."

Fury looked at the huge man who didn't flinch from anything. "Take the woman into the living area, and I want you to watch them eat every fucking bite on their plates. I don't care if they puke. They keep eating."

"You got it." The man turned toward the women. "Let's go, you fucking whores."

Traeger growled in disgust and then turned to Amelia and Tara.

"Those sluts have never eaten that much. They filled their plates for what purpose?"

Fury saw the women glance at each other before Amelia shrugged.

"We don't know."

"I think they were trying to piss you off or get back at you from this morning," Traeger guessed.

"What happened this morning?" Fury said.

"The whores were yelling at these two to make them breakfast because they woke up after the women had cleaned up."

"That fucking shit ain't going to happen."

Amelia touched his arm. "It's not a big deal."

He cupped her face and ran his thumb over her cheek. "You are here under our protection. They don't talk to you like that. Not ever."

He grabbed her hand and turned to Traeger. "Get Tara and follow."

He pulled the women into the main room over to where the whores were sitting at one of the tables with Enforcer standing there with his arms crossed over his chest.

"Listen up, you fucking cunts," Fury said. "These two women are under my protection. If I hear of any of you disrespect them like I heard you did this morning, I'll have a few of the guys take you out, beat you, and bury you."

He tightened his grip when he felt Amelia stiffen and try to pull away from him.

"Do you understand what I'm saying?"

They all nodded, and a few even started crying.

"I'm almost tempted to throw your skanky asses out. I think the boys would like some new meat."

"We'll be good, Fury," one of them said.

"This is your only chance."

Fury started towing Amelia back into the kitchen. He pulled her around and pinned her against the wall with his hands on either side of her head and his pelvis against hers. From the look on her face, he knew she could feel his hard cock pressing against her upper stomach.

"I'm warning you now. If I hear of you being disrespected, and you don't come to tell me, I'll spank your ass red and then fuck it hard enough to make it sting."

Amelia inhaled sharply and tried to push him away with her hands on his chest.

He chuckled when she got frustrated. She couldn't budge him.

She hit his chest. "What if you're the asshole that's disrespecting me?"

His eyes widened and then heated at her spunk. No one talked to him like this before, and with anyone else, he would have knocked them out. With her, it made him hotter and need her even more.

He leaned in and pressed his lips against the side of her neck. She trembled when he bit down enough to sting and then licked it.

The hands that had been trying to push him away were now grabbing at his shirt. He cupped the back of her head, tilted it up, and took her mouth in a kiss he'd been craving for weeks.

Fury wasn't known for his patience. If he wanted something, he got it, but with Amelia, he'd gone out of his way and given her time to get to know him and feel comfortable around him.

The kiss quickly turned into an inferno with both pressing against each other and his hands roaming over her body, and one hand started on her shirt.

A loud crash from the living room caught his attention, and he lifted his head.

He couldn't tear his eyes from her. Her face was flush with desire, and her eyes hazy with need. It was the most erotic thing he'd ever seen. "Fuck, babe."

He could tell the moment she realized he had her pinned, and people were walking by them.

She gasped and pushed against him. "Get back, Fury. God, you had my shirt unbuttoned."

"I would have probably had you naked in another second." He grinned when she got pissed.

"You would have been kicked in the balls if you got me naked in front of people."

He chuckled and raised a brow. "So that means I can get you naked when we're alone?"

She snorted, ducked under his arms quickly, evading his grab for her, and moved to the other side of the kitchen.

He put his hands on his hips and studied her. She was frantically trying to calm down and smooth her shirt, pretending he wasn't there.

Fury noticed Traeger was gone. Tara was at the stove, stirring a big pot and ignoring them.

He leaned against the island and smirked when she finally faced him. "It's inevitable, babe. I don't know why you're fighting it so hard."

She narrowed her eyes at him. "Nothing in life is

inevitable besides death."

He snorted out a laugh. "We'll see about that."

"Hey, boss, can you come here?" someone yelled from the living room.

Fury rolled his eyes. "Jesus Christ, it's like running a preschool." He pinned her with his gaze. "I'll be seeing you later, babe."

He chuckled when she sniffed and turned her back to him. The anticipation he felt was like a drug. He needed to be in her as far as he could and soon, or he'd go fucking crazy.

He'd see how she was later, but he already knew she wanted him, maybe as much as he wanted her. The display of passion she'd just shown him cemented his plan for her.

There was no fucking way he was ever letting her go, and the sooner she realized it, the better off she'd be.

Chapter Eleven

The chili they served that night was a rousing success, and the girls were thrilled they'd made enough for everyone to get their fill. Some was leftover for the next day or a midnight snack, too.

"Come on outside, girls, you've spent all day in here." Fury pulled Amelia out into the backyard and then picked her up.

"Put me down. I want to take a shower first."

Amelia's mouth dropped open when one of the men picked Tara up, making her scream, and dropped her in the pool. She exhaled in relief when her friend came up sputtering and cursing.

Then she smiled. Until she realized Fury was standing next to the pool, and she was hanging over it. "Don't you dare," she warned him and tried to clutch his shirt.

"Or what?" he asked with a smirk.

God, most of the time, she wanted to wipe the smirk off his face, but other times, he looked so fucking hot she just wanted to jump him.

"Or … I don't know, but it won't be good."

He chuckled. "I think I'll take my chances."

She screamed when he tossed her in.

Amelia came up spitting mad. "You shithead," she yelled at him.

She saw Tara pull herself from the pool and wring her shirt out. When she turned back, Fury was reaching over his shoulder to grab the back of his t-shirt and pull it over his head. His eyes didn't leave her as he pulled his boots and socks off.

Her eyes widened when his hands went to his pants. He unsnapped and then unzipped before slowly pulling them down and off. Fortunately, he was in dark boxers and wasn't naked.

She realized too late she wasn't close to the steps to exit, and he was ready to jump in. Screeching, she tried to race toward the steps. Two steps into her escape and an arm came around her middle and pulled her back against a hard, hot chest.

Amelia half-heartedly tried to pull his hands from her body, but it made him tighten his grip.

"Whoa, wait, babe. I want to play with you."

She snorted. "I just bet you do."

He burst out laughing.

She inhaled when one of his hands cupped her breast, and the other hand kept her pinned to his chest.

Her eyes slid closed, and her head fell back against his shoulder when he bent and sank his teeth into her neck.

"Oh, God," she whimpered.

He chuckled. "I can make you feel so good, baby. This is nothing."

"I don't know, Fury. I didn't want to stay around, remember?"

"Well, now, you don't have to worry about that because you're not going anywhere."

"You can't keep me here against my will."

"But babe, it won't be. You're going to decide to stay with me on your own."

She tried to snort, but it came out a groan when he bit down on her again.

He used his thumb to rub back and forth over one of her tits while his other hand pressed her tighter against the bulge of his cock.

It was driving her crazy as he slowly humped her from behind at the same time that he bit her shoulder and scraped across her nipple.

She was so close to actually coming she forgot the crowd of people behind them.

"You know I could pull off your jeans right now and ram into your cunt, and you'd let me. That's how close you are. Can you feel how I can take your body over and make it do what I want?"

She tossed her head against his shoulder.

"Just stop fighting me, babe. Let me make you feel good."

"Fuck, boss, I'm sorry to interrupt, but Mac at the warehouse is on the phone and said it's urgent."

"Goddammit," Fury bit out.

She roused at the anger in his tone. "What's wrong?"

"I have to take a phone call, babe."

Her eyes widened as she took in all the people staring at them. "Oh, my God," she squealed.

She tried to push his arms off her, but he just tightened them. "I'm letting you go right now, babe, but this is far from over."

"I can't believe you were touching me like that in front of everyone. They must think I'm one of the whores."

"That's fucking bullshit. Not that I care what anyone thinks, but what they think is you're my woman."

"But I'm not."

He growled and released her. "Go on and run, babe, but I'll come to get you later."

She stepped out of the pool and tried to squeeze the water out of her long, dark hair. "No, you won't. I'm going to bed."

He made her nervous when all he did was smile.

"I'm not kidding, Fury."

He tipped his head forward. "I know, babe."

She took several steps back when he pulled

himself from the water. He snatched a towel from a chair nearby and started drying his hair. "You better go on, babe. Run while you can."

She growled out her frustration, turned, and marched into the house, ignoring all the laughter and hoots.

When she got to the room, the only light on was in the bathroom. She could just see Tara's shape in the bed.

Amelia showered and then dried her hair before pulling on panties and a t-shirt. She crawled into bed and pulled the blanket up.

"How much longer do you think you can hold out with Fury?" Tara asked in a groggy tone.

"As long as I can."

Tara snorted.

A few minutes went past when Tara spoke up again. "I like it here. I feel safe, which is ridiculous because I know they're a vicious motorcycle club, but I don't think the men would ever harm us."

"I know they won't. I know what you mean. I don't remember ever feeling this relaxed or anxious for the next day to see what happens. Before we came here, I dreaded having to get out of bed."

Tara agreed.

"Do you like Traeger, Tara?"

"Yeah, but I'm not sure he likes me. I catch him staring at me, but then he ignores me when we run into each other. Then if he sees another man around me talking to me, he gets pissed."

"I've seen him stare at you when you're not looking. I can guarantee he's hot for you."

"We'll see," Tara said. "We just moved in, and I don't want to rock the boat. I feel like we already made some enemies with the women."

Amelia sighed. "Yeah, I agree. We'll just have to watch each other's backs."

"That's easy. We already do that."

Amelia reached out and squeezed her hand. "You're right about that."

"Night."

"Night, Tara."

It took a while for Amelia's mind to wind down enough for her to sleep. Thoughts of the last few days wouldn't stop crowding her brain.

The sound of the guys in the backyard helped her calm and close down enough to finally sleep.

Her last thought was of Fury and how much she wanted him, but she didn't want to want him as she did. It felt like she had no control over her body, and it scared her a little.

It didn't really matter. She knew she was going to give in to him sooner rather than later. There was no way she could hold out much longer with the way he made her feel just by touching her.

Chapter Twelve

The bedroom door opened an hour later.

Fury and Traeger stood by the bed, staring at the women.

"What did Mac have to say?"

Fury grunted. "Another shipment was lost."

"What the fuck. Who the hell is messing with us?"

"I've got some ideas but no way to prove it yet. They'll fuck up eventually, and then we'll get them."

"They've taken a boatload of money from us."

Fury nodded, and his attention went back to Amelia. "God, I want that woman so bad I ache."

Traeger grinned. "Then take her. You know she won't be able to resist you."

Fury ran a hand down his face. "I'm going to shower, and then I'll come back for her."

"I'll wait."

Fury glanced at him. "You're going to stay with Tara?"

"Yeah. I just want to hold her. I haven't held a woman for a long time."

Fury slapped his shoulder. "I think you two would be good for each other."

"We'll see. I'm not sure I can move forward yet, but my hands are itching worse than I can ever remember."

"I'm glad to hear it. I'll be right back."

Fury was back five minutes later to find Traeger leaning against the dresser with his stare on the bed.

"I'll get Amelia out of here."

Reaching over Tara, he picked Amelia up. She was so damn tiny, she was easy to move around. He grinned when she growled, tucked her nose into his neck, and then fell back to sleep.

"Night."

"Night," Traeger said and closed the door.

Fury got into his room and closed the door with a foot before moving toward the bed and laying her down. He quickly shed the boxers he'd put on after his shower and climbed in after her.

His arms wrapped around her middle and pulled her tightly against his chest.

She wiggled her ass against him, murmured his name, and then slept.

He felt a bead of sweat slide down his spine.

He thought he'd be able just to hold her, but the feel of her and her scent was slowly driving him insane.

Fury rolled her to her back and then pushed the blanket down to her hips. He ran his hand up and down her torso. His mouth settled on her, and he licked and nipped at her lips until she started to rouse.

"Mmmm."

"Open your mouth," he ordered in a hushed tone.

Her eyes fluttered open to stare up at him. "Fury?"

"Yeah."

"Where are we?"

"In our bed where we belong." He emphasized the word *our* to get her attention.

She reached up and ran her fingertips down his cheek.

"No more running from me, babe. Do you understand?"

She exhaled and nodded slowly.

"Good." He bent down and took her lips the way he'd wanted to from the very beginning.

Within a minute, they were both writhing against

each other, trying to get closer, groaning, and trying to breathe at the same time as consuming each other's mouth. He pulled the shirt up and off her before tossing it to the ground. Next, he ripped her panties away, impatient to get inside her.

He groaned, and she whimpered when he slid his hand down and slipped a finger in between her pussy lips and then up into her cunt. "Jesus, woman. You're so fucking tight."

She ran her hands over his chest and shoulders at the same time she lifted her hips.

He pulled out and then pushed two in simultaneously. Then he bent and took a nipple into his mouth. Her back arched off the mattress when he sucked hard.

"Ahh," she screamed.

"Are you a virgin?'

She shook her head.

"When's the last time you had sex?"

"I don't know, three or four years ago."

"How many men?"

A frown puckered her brow. "One. Why all the questions?"

"Because I need to know, so I don't hurt you."

He took her other nipple into his mouth as he slid three fingers into her. He needed to stretch her a bit because he was just too damn big. Even some of the whores had a problem taking him.

He hadn't realized how innocent she was, and now he started to worry. The thought he'd scare her enough to run from him made him dread fucking her, but he'd wanted her for weeks and wasn't going to put her back in her bed. He'd just have to take it slow.

She started to take his three fingers pretty well and was now begging him. He felt her cream slide out of her, making him desperate to be in her.

Fury grabbed a condom and rolled it on before moving between her legs. He cradled her head between his hands as he started to push into her.

Every time she whimpered or stiffened, he would pause.

"It's too much, Fury," she whined as her nails dug into his waist.

"You can take me, babe. We'll just go slow."

About halfway in, he reached between them and started rubbing her clit. She immediately arched up, taking more of his cock. As he kept up the assault on her clit and took her nipple into his mouth, she was thrashing and begging him.

"All right, baby. I'll give it all to you." He grasped her hip in his hand and pushed until he bottomed out inside of her.

"Ahh," she screamed and tried to push him off. "Stop. It's too much."

"Easy, babe. It will be okay. Give it a minute." He nuzzled her temple as he continued to try to soothe her. "Jesus, you're like a fucking virgin."

God. He was stunned at the thought he'd be the only man to have her for the rest of their lives. After a minute, he asked, "Are you doing okay?"

She inhaled and shuddered before she nodded. "Yes."

"All right. We'll take it slow at first."

He didn't want to scare her and tell her how close to the edge he really was, and it took every bit of his strength to keep from ramming into her.

Fury pulled out until only his cock head was in and then gently pushed back it. He did that several times until he could feel her start to move under him more. Her arms came around his waist as she tilted her hips up.

"That's a good girl." He bent and kissed her with all the passion he'd built up since meeting her, and his thrusts strengthened and grew faster. He pulled his mouth from hers and pressed it against her shoulder. Her breath caught in her chest, and her nails dug into his back, making him hiss, pushing him to go faster.

"That's it, baby. I can feel you tighten on me. Come for me."

"No," she cried. "It's too much."

"No, it's not. Don't be afraid. You know I wouldn't let anything happen to you."

The look of trust she gave him at that moment made his chest tighten with emotion, and he knew she would forever have his heart.

Her internal muscles constricted his movement so much he couldn't move, but he pushed through, giving her what she needed to go over.

"Come for me," he said with a growl.

Her scream rose until he slammed his mouth down on hers to soften the sound.

After she came down, she lay lax under him, her breathing erratic.

"Now it's my turn. Hold on to me, babe."

Her arms wrapped weakly around his neck. He held his weight off her as he powered into her at a fast rate. He was shocked and pleased to feel her tighten on him again. "Come with me."

That was all it took, and they both were flying. Their groans and cries filled the room.

He lay on her, panting and bracing himself on his elbows the best he could, but his arms shook. That fact freaked him out a bit because he'd never had that reaction before. He'd always had perfect control. He should have known it would be different with her. It had from his first look at her.

Fury rolled to the side, grabbed a tissue to dispose of the condom, rolled back, and pulled her tightly against his chest.

It took several minutes before their breathing was back to normal.

When he pressed a kiss to her forehead, temple, and then her lips, he couldn't believe he was instantly starting to harden. After the biggest orgasm in his life, he wanted more from her. He was afraid he'd never get enough. "How are you, babe?"

"I'm okay."

"Are you sore?"

He grinned when she blushed and tried to hide her face against his shoulder.

"How can you be embarrassed when I just had my cock deep inside you?"

She shook her head. "I ... I don't know. I guess I'm a little sore," she murmured against his neck.

He tipped her face up and smiled before he lowered his head and pressed a soft kiss on her lips.

"I'm going to hold you all night, and I hope every night for the rest of our lives. Can you handle that?"

"Yes."

"Good. Go to sleep."

He rolled her over to her side and spooned her before pulling up the blanket.

Fury listened to her breathing deepen before he relaxed. He pressed one more kiss to the back of her head before he closed his eyes and slept.

Chapter Thirteen

A few weeks later, the women had a routine that worked well and gave them some time of their own.

Amelia grinned. Her relaxing time was usually spent on her back or hands and knees in Fury's bed. If he caught her not doing anything, he'd pick her up, throw her over his shoulder, and take her to their bedroom. He'd done it so many times, she'd given up trying to fight or reason with him. She could still feel herself blush at all the hoots and whistles, which made Fury chuckle.

At that moment, he had her pinned on her back on their bed.

"Fury, I have to get to the kitchen and help Tara."

He growled and lifted his arm enough so she could slide out. She grinned as he grumbled like a child as she got dressed.

"Stop, you're being a baby. You've had me up here three times today."

He braced himself on one elbow and glared at her. "Did you just call me a baby?"

She bit her lip to prevent the giggle from bursting out, nodded, and took several steps back toward the door.

She squealed when he jumped from the bed. She had just gotten the door open and was running down the hall when she heard him cussing and trying to pull on his jeans.

"Goddammit, woman. You're in such trouble," he bellowed.

Amelia had just made it to the top of the stairs when she was yanked off her feet. She screamed, getting everyone's attention.

"You're going to drop me," she screeched. "Put me down."

He chuckled and pressed her to the first available wall.

"Now, do you want to tell me again what you said to me in our room?"

She shivered at his dark, threatening tone. She wasn't the least bit scared, but she always got a tad nervous because she never knew what he would do to her.

"I … I said that you're my man."

He raised an eyebrow. She knew he didn't believe her, but she kept going.

"Really?" he asked.

She nodded. "Yes. You're the only man I can ever see myself with."

His eyes narrowed, and he pressed his cock against the junction of her legs. "Go ahead."

"I wouldn't be able to find a man as handsome, smart, or loving as you, and I think I'm the luckiest girl in the world."

He nodded once. "That's what I thought you said."

She relaxed against the wall and waited for him to release her.

"But if you ever say something like that again…"

"What? I can't call you handsome?"

He snorted. "You know what I'm talking about. If you ever say it again, your ass will be a bright shade of red, and it will be hard for you to sit down for a while. Do you get me?"

She pressed her hand to her mouth when she giggled. It took her a minute to get her laughter under control before she nodded. "I understand."

He looked to the ceiling. "Jesus, what did I do to deserve this feisty, ornery woman?"

She laughed. "I guess you were just lucky."

He grinned. "Yes, I was."

He pressed a kiss to her lips and released her.

"Go on down. I'll be right there."

"Okay, babe."

His eyes narrowed on her before she turned and walked down the stairs. She couldn't keep a straight face.

At the bottom of the stairs, she noticed Bull with his arm around a beautiful woman she'd never met.

She walked over to them. "Hi, my name is Amelia."

The woman looked her up and down. "My name's Rissa, and I don't want any girlfriends."

Amelia noticed the angry looks some of the guys were giving the woman and decided to defuse the situation.

"Well, that's fine. I hope you enjoy your stay here."

"Oh, I'll be around for a good long time."

"Alrighty." Amelia turned and rolled her eyes as she walked away. She stiffened when she heard the woman comment on her big ass. After that, she heard a few men growl at Rissa. A few said something, but she kept walking into the kitchen.

The bitch was on her own now.

"Hey, girl. I'm sorry I'm late."

Tara looked over at her and grinned. "You're not."

Amelia started washing the vegetables they were going to sneak into the lasagna that night. These guys would never get any vitamins because they never ate fruit or vegetables, so the girls found a way to hide them in different things.

"I just met the woman with Bull."

Tara snickered. "I already had the pleasure."

"She said I have a fat ass."

Tara spun around. "Are you fucking kidding me? She talked about how chubby I am."

Amelia laughed. "Well, we are sisters, right?"

They fist-bumped and laughed before they got back to work.

A few hours later, the group started coming into the kitchen to get the dinner the girls made. Bull and the woman came in. She grabbed a plate and put a tiny portion on her plate.

"Is that all you're having?" Bull asked her.

"Yeah." She looked over at them. "I wouldn't want to end up looking like them."

Bull grabbed ahold of her upper arm. "What the fuck did I tell you about respecting them? You're going to get thrown out, you stupid bitch."

Amelia watched him drag her out and then saw how pissed everyone was. "Hey, don't worry about her. She's just pissed she doesn't have tits."

They all laughed and then laughed harder when she blushed.

Enforcer snickered. "How can you still blush after living here for so long?"

Tara bumped her hip with hers. "Don't feel bad. I still can't help but blush once in a while."

A few of the guys agreed and headed outside.

Amelia and Tara waited until everyone was through the line before making their own plates and then heading outside. Amelia froze when she saw one of the new whores hanging all over Fury. Women seemed to come and go with about a handful staying full-time.

Before she could say anything, he pushed her away from him violently, making her fall to the ground.

"Stay the fuck away from me or you're dead, cunt."

The woman picked herself up and angrily walked

off.

She and Tara walked over to Fury's table. She sat down by him on the bench while Tara sat across from them.

"Do you want me to kick her ass, babe?" Amelia said softly.

Fury snorted and kissed the side of her head. "No, babe. I took care of it. Besides, I don't want you to get in a situation where you could be hurt. Got me?"

She kissed his shoulder. "Yes."

Amelia had taken a bite of her meal when she heard Tara gasp. She followed her gaze and saw Traeger with his arm around the whore who had been all over Fury.

"What the hell is Traeger doing?" Amelia asked angrily and then caught the look in her friend's eyes.

Fury glanced over and cursed, which made Amelia feel better.

"Have you two had a fight?" Amelia asked her.

"No. I thought we were fine."

"He's a fucking asshole." Fury faced Tara. "Don't even look over there. You have him running scared."

"I haven't done anything."

"Yeah, you have. The same thing this one did to me." Fury pointed at Amelia with his thumb.

Amelia gasped. "What have I done to you?"

"Made me fall in love with you."

The warm feeling she always got when he said something sweet like that to her grew.

She turned to Tara. "I believe him. I see the way Traeger looks at you."

Tara pushed the food around on her plate. "He's got a funny way of showing it."

"Just you wait. If you ignore him, he'll come running," Fury said.

"He can do what he wants. We haven't made a commitment."

"But you're sleeping together every night," Amelia said.

"Not anymore." She stood, making sure she didn't look his way. "I'm going to go start on the dishes."

"I'll be right in." She watched her friend move toward the house. Then she looked at Traeger to see his gaze following her every step. That wasn't a man who didn't care. Amelia could see the love he had for her. "Can I go over and kick him?"

Fury snorted. "No, but I'll kick his ass for you."

"What about the whore?

He shook his head. "Nope, you're not touching anyone except me."

"Why do you get all the fun?"

Fury grinned, grabbed a chunk of her hair on the back of the head, and pulled her head back. "I already told you, baby. I won't allow you to be hurt." He pressed his lips tightly against hers.

Amelia stared up at him and wondered how she got lucky enough to have him.

Chapter Fourteen

"How much longer do we have to put up with that bitch Bull brought into the club?" Amelia asked Tara when she walked into the kitchen the next afternoon.

"God, I hope not long. Just about everyone hates her. Even the other whores don't like her."

"She's all over Ax right now, and last night she was on Enforcer. However, that didn't last long once he pushed her away. She fell on her ass hard."

Tara chuckled. "I think all the guys are getting sick of her too."

Amelia grabbed an apron and pulled it on. "What are we working on today?"

"I thought we'd make some more brownies. They all seemed to like them."

Amelia snorted. "Yeah, I'd say that. We'll have to make double and remember to save our guys some."

Tara chuckled. "Yeah, Traeger wouldn't stop talking about not getting one. I felt so bad."

"We'll do better, taking care of them."

"I agree."

Amelia started mixing part of the brownies. "I'm so glad you and Traeger got everything worked out."

"Yeah. Fury was right. Traeger was running scared, but for God's sake, don't say that in front of him."

Amelia laughed. "They are kind of sensitive sometimes." She was startled when arms came around her and a mouth pressed against her neck.

"Who are you saying is sensitive, babe?"

Amelia glanced at Tara and had to bite her lip to keep from laughing at the grin on her friend's face.

"We were talking about the women. It doesn't take much to set one of them off." She knew he didn't believe her when he tightened his grip on her and growled.

"Really?"

"Yup, that's my story, and I'm sticking to it."

Fury growled and bit down on her neck. "You'll pay for that later, babe."

"We're making you brownies," she said hopefully, to try to change the subject.

He snorted. "Do I get some this time?"

"Of course. Tara and I are going to do better at putting things aside for you two. You're always the last ones in."

"Because we're always working."

"I would love to know what you're both working on all the time."

"I already told you we own a warehouse. We deliver different products to the businesses around here. We also own the laundromat and the garage in town."

"Do you deliver a lot of different things?"

His fingers bit into her hips, and she could feel him stiffen in anger. "You know I won't tell you, so stop asking."

She turned in his arms, went up on her tiptoes, and pressed a kiss to his chin. "I know. I'm sorry I brought it up."

He gripped the back of her head and pressed a hard kiss to her mouth. "I'll be in the office."

"Okay." Amelia watched him leave and turned back to Tara.

Tara shrugged. "Traeger won't say anything either."

"I won't ask again. He gets all worked up." Amelia pulled her eyes from the doorway.

"I heard a few of the guys talking about a special shipment that was making them a lot of money."

"I guessed some of the things are illegal, and I'm not sure how I feel about it. I love him enough to overlook it. I just don't want any of them caught."

"Do you have anything to eat yet?"

Amelia stiffened and then rolled her eyes to Tara before she turned to confront Rissa.

"Dinner won't be ready for a few hours, so you'll have to go get your own. There are several drive-throughs down the street."

Rissa's eyes narrowed. "I won't eat that shit. I'll end up looking like you two."

Amelia sighed. She stiffened when Rissa walked over to the refrigerator and opened it. Amelia walked over and pushed the door closed.

"You're not a part of this family. You can't just get what you want."

"The fuck I can't." Rissa tried to push her out of the way to get into the refrigerator.

Amelia had had enough. "Listen up, bitch. We've put up with your bitchy behavior, but you push me one more time, and you'll be out on your ass."

Rissa threw her head back and laughed. "You really think you have that much influence over Fury?"

"I'm not saying that. I do know what he will put up with."

Rissa tried to push her out of the way again, and Amelia held on. Tara walked over and put herself next to Amelia, facing Rissa.

"Do you want to take on both of us, whore?" Tara raised a brow.

"Fuck you both. I can do whatever I want."

Rissa screeched when a hand grabbed onto the back of her hair.

"That's where you're wrong, you cunt. We've all warned you, but now you put your hands on Fury's and

Traeger's women and disrespected them. No more. You're going to get your skanky ass out of here, and if I see you again, I'll kill you."

Amelia stared at Enforcer as he dragged the woman screaming out into the living area. She and Tara ran to the door to see what was happening.

Enforcer dragged the woman halfway to the front door and then stopped. "Does anyone have a problem with this whore going? She put her hands on Fury's and Traeger's women and disrespected them for the last time."

"No, hell, I've hated the whore since she walked in," Burn said.

"Fuck, I think we should carve her up first. Just for fun," another man commented from his perch on the sofa as he played with the knife that he always seemed to have in his hand.

Amelia and Tara glanced at each other. "Holy shit," she said.

Tara shivered. "Yeah. We forget how dangerous these guys are sometimes."

"Yeah. Thankfully, they all care about the two of us."

"Yup, because that's what happens when they don't like you," Tara said as Enforcer dragged a screaming Rissa out of the club.

"I hope Bull isn't upset. I would hate to think we're the cause of it."

"No, she's the cause, Amelia. Not us."

"You're right."

Tara snickered. "Besides, he's been ignoring her, so I doubt he'll care."

"Thank God the witch is gone."

Tara grinned. "Let's get back to the brownies."

"I'm with you."

Amelia looked over and saw Fury. He must have heard the screaming and came to see what was going on. She shivered at the cold look in his eyes.

"I was going to tell you, but Enforcer got to her first."

He nodded, turned, and went back into the office.

Tara looked at her. "Holy shit."

Amelia chuckled. "Yeah, it's certainly never boring around here."

Chapter Fifteen

Amelia walked into the back door of the club with an armload of grocery sacks. "Hey, Bear, come help Ax and me with groceries."

"Coming."

They made a few trips until sacks were piled on the island in the middle of the kitchen. She started taking things out and organizing.

"Where's Fury?" she asked. She looked up when she didn't get an answer and saw Bear trying to sneak out of the kitchen. "Whoa. Tell me what's going on?"

Bear wiped a hand down his face. "It's not the way it looks."

She walked toward him with a feeling of dread.

"Where is he?"

"In the TV room. He doesn't like her. She's his ex."

"Dana? Fury's told me a bit about her. What the hell is she doing here?"

"It's nothing. Don't get pissed. They're just talking."

She ignored him, skirted past him, and made her way toward one of the back rooms. When she got a look at the couple sitting on the sofa, her stomach twisted with pain. She walked around to stand in front of them.

Fury and his ex stared up at her. They sat very close together, and her hand was on his thigh.

"What's going on?"

"We're getting reacquainted," Dana said with a smug smile.

She turned her gaze to Fury. "What the fuck?"

His face instantly darkened. "I was going to tell you it isn't what it looks like, but the fact you don't trust me pisses me off."

"Are you fucking kidding me?" she yelled with her hands on her hips. She couldn't believe Fury was sitting with a woman who had betrayed him so much. Fury had talked a little about her, but Traeger had told Tara the story about Dana fucking around with other guys while she was with Fury, and then she told Amelia.

The woman in question wasn't what Amelia expected.

She looked skanky as hell, like she'd lived a hard life, but she could also see signs of drug use from the track from needles on her thin arms. Amelia knew she was still a stripper, but she couldn't see how men thought she was attractive. She might have been once, but it was before drugs, and hard living made her look rough.

"Really, this skank is what you want?" Amelia asked.

"Hey, bitch, don't you fucking talk like that to me," Dana said.

"You want this fucking stripper over me?" Amelia asked.

"I didn't say that," he yelled. "Besides, weren't you a stripper not that long ago?"

She gasped. "So, I'm the same as her?"

Fury wiped an angry hand down his face. "I don't fucking need this shit."

Amelia kept her eyes on him, waiting and praying for him to say something, but he sat with a stern look on his face and dared her with his expression to make a big deal about the situation.

"What would you do if me and my ex sat like this on the sofa?"

"I'd fucking kill him and beat you," he shouted.

Amelia dropped her arms and swallowed several times to keep from crying in front of either of them or the group of men standing in the doorway.

"Well, I can't do either of those things, so that leaves me with one option."

"What is that?" he asked sarcastically.

She shook her head. "I hope you're both happy together." She turned and walked off, ignoring the guys who stood in the doorway.

"Amelia, wait so he can explain," Burn said.

She stopped and looked at him. "I gave him several chances."

"You know when you push Fury, he bites. You're blaming him for something he's not doing."

"You look at them and tell me they're just catching up. Fuck that, Bull."

She walked up the stairs to her and Fury's room and pulled a big bag from under their bed. Clothes were pulled out and shoved in.

A sob caught her by surprise. She pulled up the t-shirt she held to her face and cried for a minute. When she finally reclaimed some control, she continued to pack, taking everything out of the bathroom.

She couldn't take everything and would have to come back, but she got enough to hold her over for a few days. When she could talk and not cry, she'd get ahold of Tara.

At the door, she turned and stared at the bed. She thought they'd always be together, but the dream of having a family came to a screeching halt. Turning away, she pulled the suitcase behind her.

Everyone stopped and watched her come down the steps.

"Jesus, would you wait?" Ax said.

She stopped and looked at him. "For what? He made his choice."

"Fuck, it's not what it looks like," he said.

"Everyone keeps saying that, so give me a reason he would be cuddled up with his ex."

The guys looked at each other.

Ax sighed. "I can't."

She tried to laugh, but it came out sounding pathetic. "I didn't think so. I'll come for the rest of my stuff later."

Several of the bikers tried to reason with her but couldn't come up with an explanation of why. She turned one more time to see the guys staring at her. "You guys heard him. He put me in the same hole as Dana. I've never and would never have given him a reason to doubt my love."

"He was just pissed."

"Well, good, because I am too." Amelia grabbed her purse on the way out the back door where she'd parked her car. She shoved the suitcase in the back, got in, and started to back up.

She stopped abruptly when she saw Dana with a big smile on her face as she walked out the front door. When the bitch waved at her, Amelia tore out of the driveway.

She drove around for a while, looking for a place to hide for a few days until she made plans. Every time her mind went back to the picture of them cuddled together, she got closer to losing her control, and she wanted to be secure in a hotel room before she lost it.

Chapter Sixteen

Fury stormed out of the room and bellowed. "Where the fuck is she?"

His teeth snapped together as Dana walked by him and ran her hand down his ass. "If you change your mind."

"Not gonna fucking happen. Get the fuck out." He turned back to his guys. "Well?"

Traeger cleared his throat. "She just left."

"Did she say when she'd be back? And who the hell is with her?"

Traeger looked around at the other guys before he faced Fury. "She's with no one. She left for good, man. She had a suitcase and said she'd come to get the rest of her stuff later."

Fury stared at his friend and tried to understand what he just said. When it hit him, he went crazy. He picked up the nearest glass and threw it against the wall. One thing after another shattered until he stood with his hands on his hips and his head bowed as the breath billowed in and out of his lungs.

The men stood there frozen. They would duck when something came their way but otherwise stayed silent.

"You can get her back, man," Bull yelled.

Fury nodded. "You're fucking right I'll get her back, and then I'm going to beat her for leaving." He looked around the room at the destruction and shook his head. He hadn't lost it like that in a long time. "I want all of us out looking for her while the toddlers clean up this mess."

"You got it," Traeger said and started barking orders.

Fury ran to his bike and revved it up before he tore out of the driveway with Enforcer behind him. He knew the man was protecting his back and was thankful because his mind was on one thing. Finding his woman.

Several hours later, he got more desperate and angrier with every minute that went by. He cursed when his phone vibrated in his pocket, so he pulled over and shut off his bike so he could hear.

"What?" he said.

"We found her car. Do you want us to find the room and bring her back?"

He snorted. "No, I've got it. Give me the address and then watch over her until I get there."

"You got it. We're behind the motel."

Fuck, she was really trying to hide from him when he figured out where the motel was, and it just made him madder.

Enforcer waited for him.

"Ax found her car."

Enforcer nodded. "Then let's go."

Fury tires squealed as they peeled out. It took them thirty minutes to get to the motel. He pulled up next to his guys and felt something inside of him calm.

"She's in room two-twenty."

Fury parked his bike. "Thanks, guys. You can head home."

One of the guys shook his head. "We got rooms on either side of you to watch your back."

Before he could say anything, Bull said, "Boss, if you hadn't noticed, we're in Rock's county."

Jesus. He hadn't realized.

Rock and his MC club were known to do the bad shit, and Fury and his men stayed as far away from that as possible. His men ran drugs and guns, but Rock's guys ran women and children. They didn't give a fuck about anything and would kill anyone if the price were right.

His one thought was to get to Amelia as fast as he could. "I agree. Thanks, guys."

"Do you want us to get the key?"

Fury snorted. "If I can't get in that door, I've lost my touch."

They all laughed.

The group walked up the stairs. Fury waited until the guys were in their rooms before slipping his knife between the door and jamb and fiddling a few seconds until he heard the click.

That pissed him off even more. She could have been hurt so easily. The fact she'd been in Rock's county made sweat bead on his forehead. The things that man would do to her if he found out who she belonged to made him ill.

He'd thought about just picking her up and getting on his bike and going home, but he'd probably have a fight on his hands if he did that. His little woman was one of the sweetest people he'd ever known, but if he pissed her off, he better watch out because she'd cut him down.

Fury felt better knowing the guys were there to protect them, but he was still laying his gun close so he could reach it quickly. He stepped into the room, then shut and locked the door. He scanned the small room. It was dated but clean.

First, he pulled off his leather cut and then the rest of his clothes before slipping under the covers. She was on her stomach with her head facing him.

He felt like a total asshole when he saw how puffy her face was from crying. Fuck, he could have avoided all of this if he'd only told her the truth. Instead, he'd insulted her.

Fury got closer and ran his hand up and down her

back. He pushed the blanket down so he could see her and noticed the shirt she had on. Goddammit, he hated when she wore clothes, and he'd absolutely forbidden it in their bed.

He pressed a kiss to her forehead. She didn't even move. He rolled her to her back, tore the t-shirt down the middle, and then ripped her panties from her body. The light from outside made it easy for him to see her curvy body he lusted after every minute of every day.

How could Amelia think he'd want Dana after having her?

"Fury…" she murmured in her sleep.

"Yes, baby, I'm right here."

He slipped a finger into her cunt and found it wet. She tried to close her legs when he moved in between them.

"No, baby. You don't want me to leave you alone. You're my old lady, my world. I'll never let you go."

He slowly started pushing his cock into her, gritting his teeth at how tight her cunt was.

"Jesus, you feel so damn good," he murmured against her lips.

Her eyes blinked open, and she looked at him, confused. "Fury?"

He kept sliding in and out of her, not stopping and giving her a chance for the haze of lust to leave. "Yeah, it's me."

She shook her head and tried pushing him off. He almost laughed because they both knew she couldn't budge him.

"Get off me, you bastard."

He cupped her face in his hands and then shook his head. "No, baby. You're mine. You gave yourself to me."

"And I took it back."

He did chuckle at that. "You can't do that."

She hissed. "Bullshit, you can go back to the skank."

His thrusts became harder until he was slamming into her. "You fucking know I don't want her."

"No…"

"Yes. Goddammit, she came to give me information that I've wanted on a rival gang."

"And she had to sit on your lap to do it?" she said.

"We were sitting several feet apart, and I actually just sat down, but I think she heard your voice and pushed up against me as you walked into the room."

"I didn't see you pushing her away."

"Because you pissed me off when I realized you didn't trust me." He used his thumbs to wipe away the tears that ran down her temples. "It fucked me up, so I lashed out at you, and I'm sorry."

She stared at him, gasped, and raised her hips to take him deeper.

"That's it, baby. I want all of you."

He held on to her as he drove inside of her for several long minutes. The headboard pounded against the wall, and both moaned as the tension tightened. He slammed his lips down on her as a scream tore from her mouth. He didn't want the guys thinking she was being tortured and then run into the room.

When she lay limp beneath him, he fucked her until he gained his own pleasure.

It took a few minutes with him resting most of his weight on his elbows as he waited for his heart and breathing to settle. Then he slid to his side, still embedded deep inside her.

He smoothed the hair from her face. "You better accept my apology because you know it doesn't happen very often."

She sniffed and chuckled. Her hand came up to cup one of his cheeks. "I've never felt pain like that before."

He sighed. "Baby, you can get pissed if you ever see me and a woman butt-ass naked, and I'm fucking her." He caught the tears that started to fall. "But it will never happen. I love you. I'm not going to fuck this up. I promise you that."

"I love you too."

He smirked arrogantly. "I know."

She slapped his shoulder and then squealed when he rolled them back to the way they were and started pumping inside of her.

"Let's go for round two."

She wrapped her arms around him and nodded.

"I hope you're up to a marathon fuck session because I'm going to be at you all night long, babe."

She smiled. "Shut up and fuck me."

He chuckled. "Yes, ma'am." He rammed into her and rode her hard while holding her steady with his arms on either side of her shoulders.

She cried out when he bit down on her shoulder. Then he moved down to take one of her tits in his mouth and to suck strongly until she came again.

The third time, he had her up on her hands and knees.

He pistoned into her from behind several times before he pulled her ass cheeks apart to look at her tight asshole. "Fuck, I love being in you any way I can, but sometimes I need to have your total submission, woman."

"Fury…"

He laughed. "You know what I want."

He felt her relax and give herself over to him, making his love for her grow.

She sighed as he pulled out of her cunt and

immediately started pushing through the ring of muscle and into her ass, using her cream as lube. The only time he stopped moving forward was when he bottomed out inside of her.

"Fuck, babe. You feel so good."

"Fury, please."

"You need me to fuck you, babe?"

"Yes."

"All right." He pulled out and pushed in again. He did this gently, slowly gaining speed and strength until he was pounding into her.

"Fuck, babe. I need you to come."

She pressed her face into the mattress and screamed as he rode her through a hard orgasm. Then he let himself go and filled her ass with cum. When he was able to move, he took a quick shower, cleaned her up, and then pulled her tightly against his chest.

He had no idea how long he slept before he rolled her onto her back and mounted her again. "One last time, babe." He fucked her for a minute. "Or maybe two," he said and chuckled.

Chapter Seventeen

The next morning, Amelia rolled over and moaned. She turned her head to the side to see Fury grinning while he watched her with his head propped on his hand as he rested on his elbow.

She tried to move and bit down on her lip to keep from groaning. "This isn't funny," she said. "You didn't give me a break at all, and now I'm raw."

"My cock feels raw too, babe. I hope you learned your lesson about running away from me."

She scooted to the edge of the mattress before she looked over her shoulder at him and smirked. "I hope your raw cock teaches you not to be mean to me."

He laughed.

"Oh, God," she complained as she tried to stand. She took a few steps toward the bathroom and knew she looked like an old woman because she couldn't straighten without discomfort.

When Fury came up behind her and lifted her into his arms, she shrieked.

"I'm sorry, baby. Let's get you into a hot shower. That will help the muscles."

She narrowed her eyes at him. "You don't have to sound so cheerful."

He snorted as he set her down by the shower and turned the knob.

Amelia sat on the toilet and peed as he got the water going in the shower. A few months ago, she never would have peed in front of anyone, but Fury didn't want her hiding anything from him. The man didn't have a self-conscious bone in his body.

After helping her into the shower, he slid in behind her. He used her shampoo and conditioner on her hair. The washcloth she'd used the night before was still there, so he picked it up, put some body soap on it, and thoroughly washed her body.

She cringed when he touched her swollen and raw cunt with his fingers.

He glanced at her face. "I know. I'll be quick."

She nodded, knowing it wouldn't last long. "I won't be able to sit on your bike," she told him.

"I know, I thought of that. I'm having one of the guys come and get my bike, and I'll drive us back in your car. I already called them."

Fury turned her around and went over her back while she rinsed off her front.

"Here, let me wash you now," she murmured and turned, taking the cloth from him and adding soap.

Her hands ran over every inch of his body, and she would have kept going if he hadn't grabbed her hands.

"Babe, if you don't want to fuck again, you need to stop," he warned.

"Fine." It was almost impossible to pull away from his body. It was a work of art and something she'd never get tired of looking at. He was huge everywhere. Being six-foot-four inches and weighing close to two hundred and thirty pounds of solid muscle wasn't enough. His tattoos were beautiful, each in its own way.

He rinsed off and stretched for a towel, which he used quickly before helping her out of the shower, drying her off, and squeezing as much water out of her hair as he could.

While she wanted to moan at the feel of his hands on her body, she knew he'd be on her again, and she wouldn't be able to deal with that.

"Get dressed. The guys will want to stop at Fancy's to eat before heading home."

She half-listened as he talked with his guys on the phone as she quickly got dressed. After her hair was brushed out, she added a bit of makeup to hide the fact they hadn't slept.

"Ready, babe?" he called from the door with her bag in his hand.

She grabbed her purse. "Yes."

She spotted the guys as they stood by their bikes and her car. They waved at her, but their gazes scanned the area frequently.

"I get the impression everyone is nervous."

Fury opened the passenger door and then threw her bag in the back before sitting in front. He grunted as he adjusted the seat. "Meet at Fancy's," he called out before starting the car.

"Fury, what's going on?" She could feel the tension in the air and stared as the guys all went different ways.

He lifted her hand. "We're in a rival's territory, babe."

She'd heard enough since she'd been with him to know that wasn't good, especially if they weren't friendly. "Why didn't we leave last night?"

"Because I knew I'd have a fight on my hands if I tried to take you before we made up."

"I hate the thought that I'd put you all in danger."

He kissed her knuckles. "We're good, babe. I just don't want you in the middle of something. Don't worry. We're out of their county now."

She sighed and relaxed. "Good."

"Are you hungry?"

"Yes." She nodded. "I haven't eaten since yesterday morning."

They pulled up beside the guys who'd parked in front of the diner. She waited until he came around to get her and then took her hand. When he was around her, he never took his hands off her if he could help it, and she loved that.

"Hey, mama," Ax said and laughed as he held the door open for her.

She snorted. A few weeks after she'd started to live in their club, she'd taken over the cooking and cleaning with the help of the prospects and some of the club whores. Since then, the guys had started to call her mama. It had been a joke in the beginning, but when she'd taken care of a few of them who had been injured, it had stuck.

Fortunately, she didn't mind because she knew they meant it as a compliment.

Fury took the group to the back of the diner, where a large round booth and a few bigger booths sat. Those were the seats they always took. The owner of the place didn't mind because they spent a lot of money there, and she had their protection.

The town seemed to respect their seating preference. A few times they'd come in, and one of the booths had been taken, the diners always moved, and Amelia could never see any anger or resentment.

Fury had explained that very little crime happened in the town because of them. They protected the residents, and in return, the people respected the club.

He pushed her into the round one and then sat next to her while Traeger and Enforcer sat with them and the other guys sat in the other booths. They were served coffee right away, and their orders were taken. Since they often came into the place, they didn't need to look at the menu they knew by heart.

Amelia tried ignoring the stares they got from two women she didn't know and had never seen before. They got stares everywhere they went, but one of the women was blatant about it.

"Excuse me. I need to use the restroom."

Fury slid out and then helped her to stand. He pressed a hard kiss to her lips. "Mmm, maple," he whispered and grinned.

She laughed and shook her head.

Like always, one of the men went with her and stood outside. Fury was explicit about protecting her at all times. At first, it had bothered her, but now she was used to it.

At the door, she turned to Bull. "I won't be long."

"No worries, mama."

Amelia pushed through the door. She used the toilet and was washing her hands when the door opened. One of the women, the one who had rudely stared at them, walked in. She ignored her as she came to stand behind her and stare at Amelia in the mirror.

Amelia grabbed a paper towel and looked at the woman. "Is there anything I can help you with?"

The woman smirked. "I just wanted to see a whore up close."

Amelia hid her shock at the insult. "I'm not sure where you came by that information..."

"You're with the club, right?"

"I'm with one of them, but why is this your business?"

The woman snorted and crossed her arms over her chest. "I've heard about your type of women, but you aren't what I expected at all."

Amelia raised an eyebrow. "Oh, why is that?"

"You could pass for an ordinary person."

"For your information, the club are normal people too. Good people who protect this county. I don't know where you get your information, but I wouldn't be doing this again. If the guys heard you insulted me, there would be hell to pay."

The woman rolled her eyes. "Really?" she said sarcastically. "What would they do to a woman?"

"Let's just say you wouldn't get away unscathed…"

The door slammed open, and Bull stared at the two, his stare going over Amelia to make sure she was okay.

"Everything good, mama?"

Amelia looked at the fear in the woman's eyes before she walked toward the door.

"Yes, we were just chatting." She turned back to the woman. "It was nice meeting you."

"You too," she murmured as she watched Bull escort her back to the table.

"What took you so long, babe?" Fury asked when she got back to the booth.

She stood on tiptoe, kissed Fury's lips, and smiled. "Sorry, I was just talking."

"To who?"

Bull pointed at the woman that came out of the bathroom. "That bitch was talking to her, and I'm not sure what was said, but I don't think it was good."

Amelia scowled at Bull. "It was fine."

Fury cupped her chin with his hands and made her look at him. "Are you lying to me?"

She shook her head. "No. I swear. Everything's good."

"I don't like anyone fucking with you, babe."

"I know." Amelia grinned up at him and tried to get his mind off the woman. She was afraid the woman wouldn't take her seriously about how protective they were, especially over her, but they managed to get out of the diner without a fight or a fuss.

As she stared out her window on the car as they

drove home, she prayed that woman didn't talk to anyone else like that because they took protecting the old ladies seriously. Since she was the only one so far and Tara was a girlfriend who would eventually be an old lady, they were extra vigilant, and nothing usually got past them.

Fortunately, they had let the incident with the woman go. She hoped she never saw her again.

Chapter Eighteen

The next few months flew by peacefully for the most part. Amelia had gotten her routine down, and she woke up each morning excited for the new day.

One of the guys had brought another bitch, Carlee, to the club. This one was as bad if not worse than Rissa, the one Bull had brought back to the club a few months before. Her offensive comments were getting old, and she and Tara talked about saying something to Fury and Traeger about her scathing and disrespectful attitude toward them. They saw how happy Ax was and didn't want him to lose that, and they knew she'd be kicked out so quickly her head would spin.

"Is lunch about ready?" Carlee asked as she strolled into the kitchen.

She was dressed in a very short leather skirt that didn't cover her skinny ass, and her fake boobs were about ready to spill out of the tank top she wore.

Tara glanced at Amelia and rolled her eyes. The woman kept pushing them, and if one of the guys overheard, Fury and Traeger would know within minutes. They didn't want to start any trouble, but enough was enough. They'd taken her disrespect for a couple of weeks now.

Amelia stared at her. "Lunch for the guys will be ready in a few minutes, but you're going to have to figure out your own."

The ugly anger that twisted the woman's face was shocking and unexpected. "When Ax is the prez, you fucking cunts will be out of here."

Amelia and Tara froze.

"If I were you, I wouldn't be going around saying shit like that," Tara advised her.

"Fuck you."

Amelia was curious. "Where did you get the idea Ax would ever be prez?"

"Me. I think he'd make a better prez than Fury."

Amelia sucked in a shocked breath. "Have you talked to him about it?'

"No, not yet," Carlee said with a smirk.

"If I were you, the sooner you talk to him, the better," Amelia told her. She'd be interested to see what Ax said to the bitch.

"Don't fucking think you know anything about me or my life, bitch. I'm stronger and smarter than both of you put together."

Amelia chuckled. "I say one word to Fury, and you disappear, and I'm not talking about getting thrown out of the club. If you're as smart as you say, you wouldn't be disrespecting the old ladies of the club."

"Fuck that," Carlee said. "If I'm an old lady fighting with another, they'll leave us alone."

Tara set the butter knife down. "But … bitch, you're not and will never be an old lady of this club."

"Fuck you."

The back door slammed open, and several of the guys walked in. Traeger and one of the other guys stopped when they looked at the women's faces.

Traeger walked up behind Tara and wrapped his arms around her waist from behind. "Is there a problem, baby?"

Tara glanced at Amelia and then shook her head. "No, we're good."

He turned her around and pinched her chin between his thumb and finger.

"If you're lying to me and I find out, your ass will be so hot you won't be able to sit for a week."

"I'm not lying, Traeger. You know how women are."

He snorted. "Yeah, you're all bitches."

Tara slapped him in the arm. "Hey!"

"But not you, baby," he murmured against her lips.

She rolled her eyes before he deepened the kiss.

Amelia watched Ax walk into the kitchen with Bull and observed the way he and Carlee acted. She was surprised to see him ignore her, and from the look on her face, she wasn't happy about it at all.

Amelia went back to making sandwiches as fast as the men took them.

She and Tara got patted on the shoulder as the men made their way outside.

"Thanks, mamas," they all said.

Traeger had let go of Tara, so she turned back and helped Amelia.

Fury walked into the kitchen and came right to her. He gripped a chunk of her hair on the back of her head and bent her neck so he could kiss her lips. He turned her when the kiss heated, like it always did.

"Get a room," someone said.

He pulled away and stared down at her. "It never gets old kissing you. I heat up just looking at you. Fuck, all I have to do is think about you."

She cupped his cheek. "I feel the same way."

He smacked her ass, making her squeal. "You better, babe."

"Always. Now, do you want a sandwich?" she asked him.

"Fuck, yeah. Make me three."

"You got it."

Amelia peeked at Carlee through her eyelashes to see the woman's hate-filled gaze center on Fury and then her, and got pissed. She quickly blanked it when Fury glanced at her.

"Why the fuck aren't you helping them?" he asked Carlee.

Carlee raised her nose in the air. "They've got it handled."

He pressed a kiss to Amelia's forehead as he grabbed the plate she held out to him.

Fury stopped at the back door, turned to Carlee, and shook his head. "Fucking worthless."

Tara and Amelia continued to make sandwiches while they fought not to laugh at the shock on Carlee's face before it turned into hatred.

All three women jumped when the back door flew opened, and Enforcer came through. He took one look at Carlee and growled.

Carlee hadn't been able to hide her anger quickly enough. He saw it and growled. "You're not fucking looking at these two like that, are you?"

Amelia's heartbeat sped up at the anger on Enforcer's face.

"Answer me," he said when Carlee didn't speak.

"No, of course not," Carlee said hurriedly.

Amelia noticed Carlee was smart enough to be afraid. They were all scary guys, some more than others, and Enforcer was one of the most dangerous. He looked like he could walk up to you, and if you didn't say what he wanted, he'd carve you up like a Thanksgiving turkey and enjoy every minute of it. He glanced her way. "Is she bothering you girls?"

She and Tara shook their heads.

"No, everything's good," Amelia said quickly.

Burn pointed a finger at Carlee. "I'm watching your ass, bitch. I haven't liked you from the start. Why Ax gives you the time of day is beyond me. You're nothing but a fucking skank."

Carlee gasped, turned abruptly, and walked out.

Amelia and Tara continued to make the food, and Amelia could sense Enforcer staring at them for a long time, but they ignored him.

"If that bitch gives you any problem, tell me."

Both women looked up and nodded.

"Sure," Tara said. "How many sandwiches do you want?"

"Two for now."

Tara handed him a plate.

He stopped at the back door, his narrow-eyed gaze fixed on them. "If I find out she's messing with you and you don't tell any of us, I'll make sure your men punish you enough so that you won't ever lie to me again."

They both nodded and watched him leave. Exhaling, they looked at each other.

"What are we going to do?" Tara asked.

Amelia wiped her sweaty hands on a towel and shook her head. "I don't know. If we say anything, she'll disappear. I don't want to be responsible for her death."

"Me either, but I think she could pose a threat."

"Let's tell them if anything else happens, okay?"

Tara nodded. "I like that idea."

"Women, get your asses out here," a voice yelled from the backyard.

They both smiled, grabbed their own food, and walked out to see most of the club sitting at the picnic and a few round tables around on the grass.

The club had become a family to her, and she cared for each one of them. Some more than others, but she would do what she could to make their lives easier.

Chapter Nineteen

Amelia gasped when Fury pulled her onto his lap as she walked by. Fortunately, he caught the plate she'd held before it landed on the ground.

She scowled at him when he smirked. "You could have just told me where you wanted me."

"Naw, I like my way better."

She rolled her eyes when several of the guys hooted and laughed. They all ate and goofed around for the rest of the afternoon.

Amelia tried to push out of his lap.

"Where do you think you're going?"

"I have to start thinking about dinner."

He tightened his grip on her and shook his head. "No, we're ordering pizza to give you women a break."

She squeezed his face between her hands and pressed a kiss to his nose. "Aren't you the sweet one."

He growled and moved her so she lay across his lap with one of his arms supporting her.

"Sweet. You're calling me sweet," he said.

She giggled. "Yes. But in the best possible way."

Fury cupped her chin in the palm of his hand and slammed his mouth down on hers. After several minutes, he raised his head and looked around the yard while she tried to calm her breathing. She widened her eyes when she felt his hand sneak under her long skirt and then rip her panties off. She grabbed his hand. "Wait, what are you doing?" she squealed.

He grinned and pushed one finger into her.

She tried hard to push his hand away, even as the passion started to take over her reasoning.

"Men," Fury yelled. "My woman called me sweet."

Most of them laughed.

"Don't you think she should be punished for that?"

A lot of *yeah*s were yelled.

"Wait, what are you doing?"

"Don't worry. They can't see my pretty pussy," he said and grinned. "But I'm going to show them how pretty you look when I make you come."

She squirmed to get away, which made him laugh because they both knew she wouldn't get away until he was ready.

"This is so mean," she complained as she kept fighting him.

"No, what's mean is you calling me sweet."

Amelia didn't know what made her do it, but she smiled and said, "But you are sweet."

His eyes widened in shock at her playfulness, and then a warmth filled his expression. "You never cease to amaze me."

"And I hope I never will."

His mouth slammed down on hers as his finger lightly circled her clit under her skirt.

Her cunt tightened unbearably on his finger as the blood rushed through her veins, and her lungs fought to get a full breath.

"Please."

"She's begging already," Fury told the guys.

"Make her wait for it," one of them called.

She reached up and stroked his cheek. "Don't listen to that asshole," she said, making everyone laugh.

Fury abruptly rammed a finger deeper into her cunt, making her yelp.

She vaguely heard one of the guys say, "Fuck, that's hot." She knew she should feel embarrassed, but at the moment, she was too far gone to care.

"You know what you do to me?" Fury said.

Amelia stared and shook her head.

"I want to have you tied to me in every way possible."

She cried out when he shoved in two fingers, making her stretch almost unbearably. Her hand fell to his chest, where she gripped his t-shirt in her tight fist. "Please," she begged.

"I'll send you over as soon as you give me the words I want."

Her brows puckered together in confusion. "What?"

"I want the words," he whispered against the side of her head. "You know what they are."

She tried to smile, but it was hard when she was gasping for breath and writhing on his lap. "I love you."

He grinned. "Yeah, fuck yeah, you do."

The tension built inside of her until she thought she'd die from the sweet pain.

"Come for me, babe."

That was all it took to send her over. She screamed against his chest as wave after wave of ecstasy slammed into her, making her shake.

"That's it, babe. Give me everything."

Finally, she lay limply against his chest with her eyes dazed. She cried when he pulled his fingers out of her cunt, stuck them in his mouth, and sucked off every bit of it.

One of the men grunted. "Fuck, I can't take it. Where's one of the sluts?"

"I can't believe you did that in front of them," she complained after she opened her eyes.

Fury chuckled. "I think you enjoyed it as much as they did."

"I did not," she said.

"Oh, fuck yeah, you did. You came hard, babe."

"I always do with you."

"Yeah." He smiled. "But this time being watched added something for you."

She yelped when he stood with her in his arms.

"Someone order pizza in a few hours," he snapped, turned, and walked into the house.

They barely made it to their room before Fury had her pinned to the door and slammed inside of her.

"Yeah, this is my home. This little pussy. Fuck, you feel so good."

Amelia hung on as he slammed into her. This wasn't a slow ride to the top of the pinnacle. It was a ferocious feeling of flying.

"Please…" she begged.

"Yeah, fuck, come for me, babe. I won't last."

She bit down on the skin between his neck and shoulder as she came, making him shudder and follow her, filling her cunt with his semen. Then she felt nothing as she passed out in his arms.

Chapter Twenty

The next morning, Amelia walked into the kitchen to find Tara already flipping pancakes.

"Damn, you're up early."

Tara smiled over her shoulder. "Yeah, Traeger had to leave early, and I couldn't fall back to sleep."

Amelia poured herself a cup of coffee and then pulled bacon from the refrigerator. "I know how that is. I don't sleep well at all when Fury is away."

They chatted as they made breakfast, keeping it in the warm oven for when the men woke.

"Hey, thanks for the show last night," Tara said and grinned.

Amelia could feel the heat of a blush spread across her face. "Oh, God, you saw it all?"

Tara chuckled. "No, Traeger picked me up and threw me over his shoulder before you orgasmed. But I've got to tell you, Traeger was all over me, and it was so good."

"He's always all over you."

Tara nodded and smiled. "Yeah, you're right about that. It just added a little spice to it."

"I'm glad to be of service," Amelia said sarcastically, then grinned.

"Hey, I smell bacon," Bear said behind them.

Amelia snickered. "Yeah, I figured you'd be the first one in here."

"Hey, I'm a growing boy."

"Lord, if you grow any more, we won't be able to get you through the door."

"Are you calling me fat, woman?" he said.

Amelia rolled her eyes. No matter how much the guy ate, he never had an ounce of fat on him. "Seriously.

I'm talking about your height. You're six-feet-six. You already have to duck coming in and out."

He grinned and grabbed a piece of bacon off the platter.

Amelia snorted. "You better leave some for the other guys, or you're going to get your ass beat."

He shrugged. "If they woke up at a decent time, they could have some."

Both women laughed.

Amelia turned when the kitchen door swung open again. Dread filled her when Carlee walked in. She could tell right off the woman was ready to fight because she looked so pissed.

"What's up your ass?" Bear asked Carlee when he saw her.

"Fuck off," she hissed as she grabbed a cup of coffee and a handful of bacon then turned at the doorway. "I'll be seeing you."

Amelia snorted.

"Do you think she's going to share that with Ax?" Tara asked.

Bear chuckled. "That bitch doesn't know what sharing means. I wish Ax would wake his ass up, take a good look at her, and kick her ass out. She's nothing but trouble."

Amelia agreed but kept it to herself.

A few hours later, Amelia came into the kitchen with her purse.

"I'm heading to the store for a few things, is there anything you need?"

Tara looked up from the bowl of cookie dough she was stirring. "Sugar."

Amelia grinned. "Already on my list. The guys go through the stuff like it's candy."

"Do you want me to go with you?" Tara asked.

"No, I won't be long."

"Who are you taking with you?" Tara asked.

"No one. Everyone's busy."

Tara frowned in concern. "Fury is going to be pissed. You know the rule."

"If I don't go to the store now, we won't have any food for lunch or dinner. Besides, I'm wearing the cut Fury got me."

"Can you wait a bit, and I'll go with you?"

Amelia rolled her eyes. "No one is going to mess with me in town. They all know who I am."

"I hope you're right. Be careful."

Amelia grinned. "I always am."

She got in her car and left. Within ten minutes, she was pulling into the grocery store parking lot.

Amelia had just gotten out of the car when something was pulled over her face. The fear that swept through her was unlike anything she'd dealt with before, and she had to swallow the bile that crept up her throat.

She tried screaming and fighting, but within a minute, the person dragged her back and then threw her into what she assumed was the back of a van. The floor was hard metal and cold.

The person pinned her down on a rigid surface to keep her from rolling as the vehicle sped off with her inside of it.

"Tie the bitch up."

Amelia tilted her head. She knew that woman's voice but couldn't believe she would do something like this.

The cloth was dragged off her head. She blinked a few times. A young man was getting a roll of duct tape as Carlee drove.

"What are you doing, Carlee?"

"Shut the fuck up," she yelled and then laughed.

"Fuck, girl, you made that damn easy. I thought we'd have to knock one of the guys out to get you."

Amelia looked at the man and knew he wasn't old enough even to drink.

"Hun, you don't want to do this."

"Hush, if you don't fight, I won't hurt you."

She saw the worry on his face and then caught the patch he had on his cut.

"You're one of Striker's prospects?" Hell, the guy couldn't be older than nineteen.

"Yeah."

"Did he tell you to do this?"

"No, Carlee said Striker would be thrilled."

"Oh, God, honey. This is a death sentence."

The kid turned her around and taped her wrists together behind her back.

Amelia tried again. "She's going to get you killed."

"My club will protect me," he said.

"No, you don't understand. It's your club that's going to kill you. Do you really think your prez will be happy that you're starting a war with the Devils?"

The guy's hold tightened on her as Carlee took a curve too fast.

"A war?" He swallowed.

"Yes. I'm Fury's old lady. He's the Devil's prez."

He froze, and his mouth dropped open. Then he turned to Carlee. "You said she was one of the whores that betrayed Striker."

"Shut the fuck up," Carlee screamed. "And don't listen to her. Put some tape over her mouth."

"What's your name?" Amelia asked him.

"Tag."

She glanced at Carlee and saw she was concentrating on the road before looking back at the kid and whispered, "Listen, I will do whatever I can to keep you alive. You should have never been involved with something that woman did. She's extremely good at manipulating people."

"Do what I said, fucker," Carlee said. "I don't want to ever hear that woman's voice again."

"I'm sorry," Tag said. "I won't put it on tight."

She nodded. "It's okay. Do it."

Chapter Twenty-One

Amelia tried to calm herself enough to get her thoughts in order. When she was in front of Striker, she would plead for Tag's life and convince Striker to let Fury have Carlee. She felt better having a plan in place, and she prayed things would go smoothly and no one would get hurt.

"We're here," Tag whispered. "I don't know what to do."

Amelia heard the terror in the young man's tone and wanted to reassure him, but there was no time, and she was still gagged.

The side door of the van opened.

"Get her the fuck out."

Amelia almost rolled her eyes at Carlee but tipped her head at Tag to indicate to follow Carlee's orders.

Tag gently helped her out of the van.

She flinched when Carlee took ahold of her arm and yanked her along. Amelia stumbled a few times, but Tag was there to catch her before she fell.

Amelia's fear tried to take over, but she pushed it back as everyone in the room stood, and a deadly silence grew. Jesus, they had to have thirty guys right here.

Within a few minutes, two huge men pushed through the crowd to stand in front of them.

It didn't take long for Striker to guess who she was because of the vest she wore.

"Why the fuck do you have the Devil's Sons' prez's old lady in my fucking house tied up?" His voice got steadily louder and colder.

Carlee stepped toward him and pushed Amelia. Striker caught her gently and held her arm to keep her from falling.

She shook her head. "Mmm-mm-mmm." She tried to get his attention.

Striker turned her toward him and gently pulled off the tape. "I'm right that you're his old lady?"

Amelia nodded. "Yes. Can I talk to you?"

His eyebrows rose, and he gritted his teeth. "Talk here."

She sighed and looked around at the crowd.

"This was all Carlee's idea. She thought you'd be pleased having me in your hands. She was hoping you'd kill me. My new friend Tag was manipulated by the best and tried to protect me."

"Shut her the fuck up," Carlee screeched.

Striker glared at Carlee. "Tony and Feral, hold the whore and shove something in her mouth if she yells again. And I want a few others to hold Tag."

He looked back down at Amelia. "Go ahead."

She cleared her throat and looked around again. "I've got some ideas, but I won't say them in front of everybody. Please."

Striker sighed. "Blood, come with us. The rest of you hold tight until I get back."

Striker walked her back to what she assumed was his office.

"May I have my hands untied? They are starting to go numb."

"Fuck," Striker said, likely just realizing it.

"I got it, boss." Blood pulled a lethal-looking knife out of his pocket and cut the tape.

"Thank you, Blood."

Both men looked shocked for a moment.

"There's no reason to be rude. I'm just trying to be polite, guys." Amelia moaned at the pain that raced down from her shoulders from having her arms tied behind her back.

"Fuck, lady," Striker said. "I'd help you, but I'd have to put my hands on you, and I'm already a dead man."

She smiled and shook her head. "No, you aren't. I want to ask a big favor."

"Seriously?" Striker spit out with wide eyes. "Right now?"

"Well, it's actually two."

He crossed his arms over his chest. "Go ahead."

"The first one is I don't want you to kill Tag."

"He could have started a fucking war, lady."

She frowned at him. "My name is Amelia, not lady."

Striker rolled his eyes, and Blood grinned.

"Carlee is a horrible person and has hated me from the time she showed up at our clubhouse."

"When was that?"

"About three months ago, I think."

"She's been here about a month."

Amelia's eyes widened. "She was playing both clubs."

"Fucking cunt. She'll pay for that."

"That's another request I have. I want you to give her to Fury."

"Fuck no," Striker said. "She could have gotten my whole club killed."

"And also, mine, but she didn't take your old lady, and that's what this is going to be about."

"What do you expect us to do with Tag, pat him on the back?" Blood said sarcastically.

She snorted, making both men's eyebrows raise again. "No. I know better than that. Could you just beat the crap out of him instead of killing him? I can guarantee he's already learned his lesson."

"Why are you pleading for one of my guy's life?"

"Because if he had been older, he would have known better. He's just a kid. Haven't we all been through betrayal and trusted someone we shouldn't have?"

Both men looked pissed but nodded. "So, you want me not to kill the kid and give you that whore?"

She smiled and nodded. "Yes. Please. I promise to do everything in my power to settle the Devil's Sons down before a fight starts."

"You have that much influence over the men?" Striker asked, surprised.

"Oh, hell, no. But if I can get Fury's attention, he'll control them."

Striker and Blood exchanged looks and seemed to come to an understanding.

"Fine." Striker sighed. "How do you want to play this?"

"Let me call Fury and explain and then set up a meeting."

"I want to be in the room when you call."

She nodded and smiled. "Of course."

She almost laughed at the confusion on their faces. She could tell they didn't know how to deal with her, and it was funny. They must be used to hard, coarse women and hadn't been around one who was soft and gentle.

"Come here," Striker said. He walked around his desk and lifted the phone.

She stood on the other side of the desk with her back to them, dialed the number, and waited.

"What?" Fury asked.

"Hey, babe."

"Where the fuck are you?" he bellowed loud enough to break windows.

"It's a long story. Will you promise to let me tell

it before you freak out?"

"Woman, I've got everyone out looking for you. I've been half out of my mind with worry. I'm about ready to lose it, so you better fucking hurry."

"Carlee kidnapped me and took me to Striker's. She thought he'd be happy, but it freaked him out."

"You're where?"

Amelia sighed at the soft tone of Fury's voice, knowing he was beyond pissed.

"Listen, he wants me off his hands as quickly as possible, so I suggest we meet, and I come to you. He's also giving you Carlee, which I thought was sweet because he really wants to kill her himself."

"Has anyone touched you?"

She snorted. "No, they are acting like I have the plague."

"Good."

There was a moment of silence.

"Tell him to bring you and Carlee to the county line. Be there in thirty minutes."

"Okay, babe. I can't wait to see you," she said. "Oh, and I still have to go to the store."

Another deep growl came over the phone.

"Yeah, about that. You broke a rule of mine, didn't you?"

"I did, and I'm sorry."

"You know what's going to happen, right?" Fury asked.

"Yes. I'll be punished."

"You're fucking right, you will."

"Okay, I'll see you soon. Oh, babe?"

He sighed. "What?"

"Can we maybe do this without any bloodshed? This club didn't do anything. It was all Carlee. When they found out, let's just say I thought a few of them would have a stroke they were so pissed."

He chuckled. "Fine, I'll hold the guys back, but one wrong move and Striker is gone."

"I'll tell him."

Fury hung up.

Then she set the phone down, stood, and turned to face them. She looked at both men and sighed. "So, he said…"

"Lady, we heard everything," Blood said and grinned.

Her eyes widened.

Striker chuckled when she frowned at them. "You two have great hearing."

Both men grunted.

"I've got a question."

Amelia turned to Striker. "Yes?"

"When he punishes you, does he ever…"

"Ever what?" she asked, confused.

"Hurt you?"

She smiled. "No, Fury would never hurt me. I won't be able to sit down comfortably for a while, and after, the devil likes to smack my red ass when he passes just to remind me, but otherwise, he wouldn't hurt a hair on my head."

Striker nodded and opened the door.

"Where in the hell did he find you?" Blood asked.

She snickered. "I was a stripper."

Both men threw back their heads in laughter.

She grinned. "Yeah, I know. Most people don't believe me. I was really bad at it."

"I don't believe you," Striker said.

"Maybe I'll tell you on the way to the meeting."

He nodded.

Chapter Twenty-Two

The group was still standing in the large living area and waiting.

"Take Tag out back and…" Striker looked down at Amelia and sighed in disappointment. "And beat some sense into him but don't kill him and no broken bones because I'm going to put his ass to work."

"You got it, boss."

Two of the men with Tag in between walked her way.

"Bye, Tag."

He stopped by her. "Thank you, ma'am. I owe you my life."

She shook her head and patted his cheek. "No. Growing up is hard enough. Just take care and be a good soldier for your prez, and I'll be happy."

"Yes, ma'am."

When she turned back, everyone was staring at her. "What?"

Striker and Blood snorted.

"We're going to meet the Devil's Sons at the county line and give Amelia and Carlee to them."

A guy standing off to the side grinned. "Why can't we keep both? I really want to get my hands around Carlee's neck and cuddle with her."

There were a few snickers in the group.

Amelia shook her head. "Not going to happen, sir. I'm sorry. I have to get back to my man. I wish I had more time to get to know you all, but my guy is pissed off enough. You all take care."

Amelia followed Striker out of the building but heard Blood talking behind her.

"Is she for real?" someone asked Blood as he

followed behind her.

"Yeah. Fury's a lucky son of a bitch."

Two men followed Blood holding a struggling, gagged Carlee.

About twenty guys got on their bikes, and Striker, Blood, and Amelia were in an SUV. A few guys had Carlee in another.

Amelia answered their questions as they drove, but her thoughts were on Fury.

"Fuck, they're already here," Blood said.

Amelia looked between the front seats to see most of her club lined up with their bikes behind them.

Oh, shit, she thought.

Striker and the other SUV pulled up in the middle of the street about thirty yards away, and the bikes branched out from there.

Striker opened the back door and led her up in front, where she stood between Striker and Blood.

Fury shook his head when she smiled and waved at him.

Fury and Traeger started to walk into the middle. Striker, his vice-prez—Blood, Amelia, Carlee, and two other guys that had ahold of the woman walked to meet them. They stopped about ten feet away from each other.

Fury's gaze raced over her, likely looking to find any injuries. When he was done, he tipped his head. "Get over here," he said with a growl.

"Okay." She turned to Striker. "Thank you for taking care of me."

"Lady, do you have a death wish? Because I don't," Striker said.

"No, why do you ask?"

"Because Fury is about ready to lose it."

She looked over her shoulder and saw what Striker was talking about. Fury's blue eyes were hard and cold, and a muscle in his jaw had a tic.

"You're right. Bye." She walked straight to Fury and looked up at him.

"Hi, babe," she whispered and smiled.

She caught the twinkle in his eye before he wrapped her up in his arms. He tucked his face against her neck and inhaled while she did the same. "Never again, baby. You will never go anywhere on your own again," he said against her ear.

"I won't, I promise."

"You scared the fuck out of me."

"I'm sorry," she murmured against his head.

Someone clearing their throat and got their attention.

Fury put her down and pushed her behind him before facing Striker.

"Your woman is making me give you Carlee," Striker said with a smirk.

Fury grunted. "That's good. I've got a beef with the cunt." He smirked. "You never had a chance with my girl. If she wants something, she usually gets it."

Amelia jerked on his cut. "That's not true."

"It sure the hell is," Fury said over his shoulder.

Fury waved a few of his guys forward to take Carlee off Striker's guys' hands. Everyone moved away, leaving Fury, Traeger, Amelia, Striker, and Blood.

"I want to make sure you know we had nothing to do with this. We don't mess around or try to hurt women or children."

Fury nodded. "Yes. We're the same way."

Striker stopped them as they turned to leave. "Hey, Fury, your woman doesn't happen to have a sister, does she?" Striker asked.

Fury wrapped an arm around Amelia's waist. "I'm afraid not."

"Damn. I imagine she keeps you on your toes."

Fury grinned. "You have no idea. But she's worth it."

The other guys walked back to their vehicles, and Fury turned them to walk back to their side.

"What does he mean about me having a sister?"

Striker must have heard her because he laughed the same time Fury did.

"I'll explain later."

"All right," she said.

Fury boosted her up into the front seat of the SUV and got in the driver's side. He lifted her hand and held it as he drove them back to the club.

"How mad are you at me?" she asked.

He smiled at her and squeezed her hand. "Very."

She narrowed her eyes on him. "Really? You don't seem angry."

"Because right now, I'm just glad to have you back. You have no idea what hell I went through when the cop called and said he found your purse lying on the ground by your car. Then a few people stepped up and told him they saw you pulled into a black van."

At a stoplight, his gaze ran over her again. "Are you sure you're all right?"

She laid the side of her head on the back of the seat so she could look at him. This big hulk of a man scared the hell out of most people with his dark looks and tattoos, but she only saw the handsome man who turned her on.

"Baby, I asked you a question."

A grin spread across her face. "I'm fine. I promise."

He glanced her way before turning his attention to the road again. "What are you staring at?"

"You. I'll never get tired of looking at you."

He snorted. "That's not going to get you out of trouble."

"I know, and I'm not saying it for that. You know, you were the first thing I thought of when a bag was put over my head."

She watched a dark, murderous look cover his face. "I thought of you, and if something happened to me, it would make you sad, and I hate that."

He pulled into the driveway at their club, twisted the key, and turned toward her.

"I love you so much, and I have to tell you it would go way beyond sad, baby. It would destroy me, so next time you take a chance like you did today, I will come down on you as you've never seen. Got it?"

"Yes. I'm sorry."

He lifted her hand and kissed her knuckles. "I know you are, but you're still being punished."

"I know, and I accept it."

He nodded and came around the vehicle to lift her out. Then he grabbed her hand and pulled her along behind him.

Several of the club whores who had befriended Amelia and Tara rushed up to her and hugged her.

"I was so worried about you," Tara said and wiped a tear off her cheek.

"Everything's okay."

"Ladies, you can all talk later. Amelia is going upstairs to our room and staying there until I come to get her."

Amelia looked up at him. "Are you going to take care of..."

He gave her a hard kiss and slapped her ass. "All you have to worry about is minding me. I'll take care of the rest."

"What if I want to say something to her?"

"It's my job as your man to protect you and take care of all things that harm you. It's your job to take care of me."

She bit her lip and nodded. "Do you know how long you'll be?"

He tipped her chin up with a finger. "As quickly as I can, but you won't come out of the room until I get you." He lifted a brow.

She shook her head. "Of course not."

"Go on," he murmured and nudged her toward the stairs.

She took one more look at him before ascending the stairs. As she walked down the hall and into their room, her thoughts turned to Carlee.

She knew what was going to happen to the woman, not to what extent, but the woman would be dead and buried before the night was over, and she didn't know how she should feel about it.

Sighing, she looked out the back window. She was able to see all the tables, swimming pool, and part of the huge Morton building where the guys fixed their bikes. Beyond that was a tall wire fence that had barbed wire at the top.

Fury did everything he could to make sure his club was safe.

A shiver took over her body as the ramifications of the day started to bleed into her mind.

She stripped quickly and showered. After she dried her hair, she put on lotion and a little nightie. Nothing she could do would keep him from punishing her, but she also needed to have him take over her body and take away the feelings that kept growing inside her.

A knock at the door startled her before she grabbed her robe and opened it.

"Fury said I could bring you some dinner, but I

can't stay and talk."

Amelia smiled. "Of course not. I'm in time-out."

Tara chuckled, set the tray on the dresser, and turned toward her.

When Amelia saw her friend's eyes mist over with tears, she pulled her into her arms. "I'm so sorry I scared everyone. I should have listened to you when you told me to take someone with me."

"I think we both learned a lesson today. I don't want you to worry about the kitchen. A few guys and I are going to the store."

"Oh, the list is in my purse… Oh, my God, where's my purse?"

"We got it back from the cop who found it."

Amelia exhaled in relief. "Thank you for being here, Tara."

"Always."

After Tara closed the door and walked away, Amelia thanked God for the people he'd brought into her life who cared about her.

Chapter Twenty-Three

Several hours later, Fury walked into his room to see Amelia sprawled out on the bed, hugging his pillow. The covers were pushed down to the bottom of the mattress, and her nightgown was shoved up over her ass, giving him a view of one of his favorite parts of her.

He caught sight of the tray Tara had brought up and noticed Amelia barely ate any of it. Since he hadn't eaten, he fed himself the rest before he pulled off his clothes. He'd already showered at the site and had his clothes burned, so he was coming to her clean. The only things left were his anger and resentment that he'd had to kill a woman.

A few of the guys took care of her body, so he knew no one would ever find her. The fucking bitch had spewed so much shit, and she kept going as they tortured her until she couldn't talk anymore. Then she just begged to die.

He wiped a hand down his face as he stood over the bed. He didn't enjoy hurting women, but sometimes it was necessary, like the one he just took care of. Nothing but death was where cunts like that belonged. She was poison to so many people and had the ability to ruin people's lives.

If she had been remorseful, they would have made her death quick and painless, but she hadn't been. It had made it easier for him knowing she had planned for Amelia to be hurt, raped, and killed. She'd told him that several times.

Fury slid into bed with his mouth starting at her ankle and moving slowly up. A chuckle escaped when she finally came awake when he was over her ass.

"It's about time." He pinned her to the mattress

when she tried to roll over. "Oh, no. You're in the perfect position for your punishment."

A tingle of awareness slid down his spine when she murmured his name and tried to get closer to him. He grinned as he ran his hand up and down her body. Starting at her neck and then down to the back of her knees.

"Fury," she whispered.

"Yes, baby, it's me."

When his hand came back up, he slipped it between her legs. He groaned. "You are always wet for me."

She nodded and tried to arch her back to get his touch to deepen.

A squeal tore from her throat when his hand came down on her ass several times before he'd trail his fingers over the red marks.

"This is such a pretty color." He chuckled when she growled.

He kept up the punishment for another minute until she was trying to squirm away, crying.

Only when he thought she'd had enough did he pull her into his arms and hold her tightly against his chest.

"You won't ever do that again, will you?"

She shook her head against his shoulder as she cried.

"Shh. That part of the punishment is done." He trailed his hand over her back, trying to soothe her.

She raised her head and sniffed. "There's more?"

"Yeah, but what I do next will mostly give you pleasure."

He rolled her back onto her stomach and grinned when her eyes closed. He felt a shiver course through her body as his finger delved in between her ass cheeks and then deep into her ass.

She gasped.

"You like me in your ass, don't you?"

She hesitated for a moment. Then she nodded and tried to get him to go deeper.

He pulled out and smacked her already tender ass cheek before pushing two fingers in her. He hadn't gotten a lot of her cream to use as lube, so he was going in harder than normal.

"Oh, God, Fury, that stings."

"I know." He pulled out and got a little more of her essence before trying three fingers inside of her.

"Take them, baby. You know you can. Relax your ass."

She murmured something and tried to loosen, and when she did, he went deeper.

He finger-fucked her until she was whimpering and begging.

"You want me to fuck your ass, babe?"

"Oh, God, yes," she moaned.

He chuckled. "I'll be right back."

After he washed his hands, he grabbed a condom and lube. He put a generous amount in her before pulling her hips up, so she was on her knees with her head and shoulders on the mattress at the end of the bed.

He would be able to control her better by standing and gripping her hips. He lined his cock up.

"Are you ready?"

"Please," she begged.

With one hard thrust, he bottomed out inside of her.

"Oh," she screamed. He knew her well enough to know that definitely was not a sound of pain.

He held her steady as she became accustomed to his cock.

"Here we go, baby." He started gently and slowly gained speed and force until he pounded into her. The thoughts he'd had earlier when he couldn't find her began to take over. He had never felt that type or depth of fear before in his life, and he'd gone through so many things that could have killed him through his lifetime.

His teeth snapped together as he fought to gain the control he needed so he wouldn't hurt the most precious thing in his life. "I don't think I'm going to be able to let you leave the clubhouse for a while."

She whimpered and tried to thrust back against him.

He smacked her ass. "Did you hear me, babe?"

She shook her head and tried to fight to get him to fuck her like she needed at that moment.

He sighed. They'd discuss it again when she wasn't so aroused or tired.

One of his hands slid around her torso to cup her breast. "Fuck. I love these tits."

Amelia's movements became more frantic, and the sounds she made got louder and needier. "Please," she begged.

He grunted. "Not yet. I want you to need me as much as I need you."

Her hands fisting the blanket under her tightened. "I'll always need you."

"That's right, you will." He thrust a few times. "This is part of the punishment. I'm going to make you hold out for a bit."

"I'd rather be spanked."

He chuckled. "I know."

The torture continued for several minutes until she was sobbing and uncoordinated.

"All right, babe. Come for me."

A sound like a whimper grew until it bounced off

the walls, and then her scream tore out of her throat.

He gritted his teeth as her ass throbbed around his cock, pushing him over.

"Ah," he groaned. His thrusts slowed until he was pumped dry.

A chuckle burst from his mouth when he pulled out of her and she fell bonelessly to her side.

"I love it when I fuck the sass and energy from you. It means I did it right." He pressed a kiss to her shoulder before he stood up. "I'll be right back."

He returned with a washcloth after he cleaned himself and slowly wiped both his and her cum, lube, and sweat from her body. After tossing the cloth back into the bathroom sink, he slid in beside her, arranged her back against his chest, and wrapped an arm around her waist.

"You're mine," he breathed against the top of her head.

"Mm, and you're mine," she whispered back, making him smile.

"That's right, babe. I'm yours too. Forever."

The End

#

Devil's Sons MC, 2

Lila Fox

Copyright © 2021

Chapter One

Tara grabbed her bag, stepped off the bus, and dragged herself the few blocks to the strip joint where she worked. She prayed it wouldn't be long before she could quit because never in a million years would she have thought she'd become a stripper.

She couldn't remember being this tired in her life, and she didn't know how much longer she'd be able to keep up without breaking. At the moment, she didn't have a choice.

A few months before, she had worked in an office as a secretary until her mother's disease had gotten worse. Then she had to get a better-paying job while working fewer hours, and it had to be at night when she had someone to take care of her mother.

Two things about the situation made what she was doing bearable. One, she loved to dance and had taken lessons from the age of three until high school. Two, she met a woman who became her best friend.

Amelia was the sweetest person Tara had ever met, and she was extremely protective of her. The night they met the biker who was interested in Amelia, she'd watched the two together, and the possessive look on the biker's face frightened Tara.

She faced him after her friend walked away. "Hey, um, mister." It took all her courage to face the guy who had to outweigh her by over a hundred pounds. He had an extra twelve inches, making him loom over her.

Fury turned toward her from Price.

Tara looked back and forth between the men and swallowed hard. "I ju … just wanted to tell you that Amelia is my friend and she's a very nice person. She's not going to w … w … want to be one of those girls in your club that … that…"

"Fucks every guy?" Fury asked helpfully and with a grin.

She cringed with a fiery blush covering her face. "Yes. That. She's gone through so much. I don't want her hurt."

"Tara's a lot like Amelia, and both pretty much have the same story," Price told him.

"How about if I promise not to hurt her, and there's no way any other man will ever put his hands on her as long as she's with me? Will that help calm your fears?"

She shrugged. She knew she would have no say in what happened, but she wanted the guy to know Amelia was loved and Tara was looking out for her.

****

The woman after the one Fury was hot for danced and caught Traeger's full attention.

Fury's woman was hot, but this one made his pulse kick into high gear. He hadn't felt this type of attraction since… Well, never.

"She's a hot little woman," Traeger murmured to Fury, who had come back and sat after meeting the woman.

"She's Amelia's friend. Her name is Tara, and they are a lot alike. If you want dibs on her, you better make it quick. I have a feeling from the looks on our brothers' faces, a few of them might try to snatch her up."

Traeger watched the woman's moves and how the men went wild for her. He could tell how self-conscious she was, but she was a good little dancer. "I need to know more about her. I'll have Franky do a background check on both."

Traeger caught Fury's conversation with Price and asked Fury, "What are you thinking?"

"I'm finding myself being protective over both women."

Traeger frowned. He'd never heard his friend say that kind of shit. "Why?"

Fury shrugged. "They're unlike any woman I've ever known. You'll see when you meet them. Their eyes are clear and full of innocence. I feel calmer when I'm with them, and I've got no fucking clue why."

Traeger turned his attention back to the stage where another woman came out. This one was grossly skinny, and it looked like every joint in her body stood out starkly. He could tell she enjoyed her job by the way she hung over the stage, getting closer to the men. He also guessed he could have her any way he wanted her, but, like Fury, Traeger was sick of fucking the same cunts as dozens of other guys had.

His thoughts went back to the woman, Tara. He guessed she'd been wearing a wig because no woman's hair was that ugly, but her facial features were smooth and delicate. She was one of the most feminine women he'd ever seen, and the way she moved was beautiful, something he could watch for hours.

Her looks, her moves, and her very presence claimed her as an untainted woman, and that was something he could never remember being around.

To meet a woman who wasn't out for herself or enjoyed the pain of others was crazy. Now he had to see if enough time had passed since horrifically losing his girlfriend right in front of him so that he could move on.

Chapter Two

Tara dragged herself off the bus the next day. Damn, she was tired. It was getting harder and harder to take care of her mom.

The night before, her mother had been especially hard, and it had kept Tara up most of the night. She'd finally come to the conclusion she was making her mother's life harder and not better by keeping her at home and trying to take care of her herself.

The place the doctor had recommended knew how to deal with people with this disease, and they knew how to handle them, could give them medication that helped, and had locks on the doors that prevented the patients from getting lost.

Tara would continue to work at the strip joint because of the money, but she'd get a job in the daytime to help pay for the bills. She just wanted to get through tonight without passing out and hope and pray her mother slept through the night.

Seated in her chair, she concentrated on her makeup. The longer she went without sleep was when she needed it the most.

Amelia sat down next to her and grabbed her hand. "She had another bad day?" Amelia asked.

Tara blinked back the tears that filled her eyes. Amelia was the only one she could talk to about her mother. All of her and her mother's friends had faded away because they hadn't wanted to deal with her sickness.

"I'm moving her into the home sooner than I thought."

"Oh, wow. That's hard."

Tara nodded.

"You'll be able to see her anytime, right?" Amelia asked.

"They said I should call before every visitation, and if she had a good day, that I could come see her, but if it was a bad day, it's better that I stay away because it might agitate her more."

They both jumped when the guy from the night before got their attention. Tara listened as Amelia talked to the guy and cringed a few times at what she said to him. She had the urge to place her hand over her friend's mouth, and she was pleased when instead of getting pissed, he smirked and crossed his arms over his chest.

"Are you kidding me right now?" Tara hissed in Amelia's ear. "He's going to smash us to smithereens."

Tara caught sight of the other man she'd never seen before, but she was concentrating on Amelia, who continued to struggle with her.

"Have you decided?" the guy asked.

"Decided what?"

"Who's going to deal with me?"

Tara rolled her eyes when Amelia asked him who was he there to see.

"You."

Tara's teeth snapped together when Amelia grinned at her and said, "Ha."

"That doesn't mean I'll let you get hurt because I'm not," Tara almost yelled.

The first guy got their attention. "Girls, this is Traeger. He's my vice prez."

Tara glanced at Amelia, hoping she'd understand what that meant, but she looked confused.

Both men grinned.

"But you're still standing here. You have to go," Amelia told him when he reminded them they needed to get ready

"Babe, you're going to be showing a lot of men your body shortly."

Tara watched Amelia explain they had to change.

"All right, go ahead," Fury said.

"I'm not doing it in front of you," Amelia yelled.

Tara cringed.

"I'm not leaving," the first biker said.

Tara almost laughed when Amelia stomped her foot and then shouted. "Yes, you are."

He rolled his eyes and straightened. "If you want, I can help you."

Tara's eyes widened. "Oh, shit. He means it, Amelia. Hurry. I'll block you, and you can get dressed and then do the same for me."

"Good idea."

Within a few minutes, both of them were dressed, and then they stood in front of him and smiled in satisfaction.

Both guys laughed, and then Fury pulled Amelia into his arms and kissed her before he nudged her toward the stage where she was supposed to start her set.

Tara turned, and her gaze was stuck on the other biker. He was just as big as Fury and had the same number of muscles and tattoos, but his hair was a medium-blond and a little longer, and he had beautiful green eyes.

"I'm going back out front," Fury told Tara.

Tara nodded and watched Fury and Amelia walk away. She fidgeted as the Traeger's steely gaze locked on her, and then he smiled.

She inhaled sharply when he took steps to stand in front of her. He cupped her chin in his palm and caressed her cheek with his thumb.

"You're very pretty."

The sound of his deep, dark tone sent a shiver

down her spine. She blushed when she saw him smile at her reaction to him. She tried to tug her head away, but he just tightened his hold.

"I think we'll get to know each other better."

She shook her head slowly. She couldn't handle a guy like this. The last boyfriend she had was in high school, and he'd been a nerd.

Traeger just nodded, and his smile grew.

She shook her head again.

"We'll see, babe." He turned and walked off. It was only when she started getting dizzy that she realized she'd been holding her breath.

She exhaled and rubbed the ache that had started in her stomach. God, if he made her feel like this after a few minutes, she couldn't imagine what it would be like after an hour or more.

Tara turned toward the mirror to adjust and straighten her wig before finishing her makeup.

"Tara, you're up."

She walked to the back of the stage and made sure all her girly parts were in the costume before heading toward the stage. She fist-bumped Amelia as she was coming off.

"Good luck."

Tara grinned. "Thanks, I'll need it."

She reminded herself to take it day-by-day and sometimes, minute-by-minute when it started to overwhelm her.

Chapter Three

Several days later, Traeger was in the shop working on his bike, trying to get his mind off the woman whose face he couldn't get out of his head.

Since he'd met Tara, his emotions had been in turmoil. Something he'd never admit to anyone. Flashes of his last girlfriend kept his guilt fresh, like it had just happened days ago instead of years.

Another part of him knew he wasn't good enough for her. He'd grown up without knowing who his father was and having a mother who cared nothing for him. Her worry had been how to get her next fix and usually whored herself to get what she needed. She didn't care if her three-year-old had gone without food for a few days.

He could remember walking into school with a ripped t-shirt and jeans because he had nothing else. If he hadn't been a badass, he would have been bullied. But if someone looked at him wrong, he'd shove them into a locker or punch them in the nose.

He jumped a few grades just to get out, but he was also determined to at least graduate high school. For a while, he'd thought about college because he thought that would be his ticket to bettering himself. Instead, he ran into Fury, and they had hit it off. After a short period of time, they had started the Devil's Sons MC club, and he'd been happy with his choice.

Now he was looking at a beautiful woman who could fit in anywhere, someone who was sweet and cared about others. He wasn't used to it. He'd never had a woman like that in his life, especially one who could only be his, ever. His mother, girlfriends, the women, and the whores he'd come into contact with over the years were so different from Tara. He hadn't realized how awful some of them were because he'd never been around a decent one.

Besides the fact he hadn't gotten over his girlfriend, Traeger didn't know if he had it in him to take care of someone like her. The guilt couldn't seem to leave him, but he wasn't sure if he was ready to move on.

He was working on his bike when Fury found him. "Is she settled?" Traeger asked.

He had helped Fury move Amelia into the clubhouse earlier and was curious about how she was taking the environment.

"Yeah, she's out."

Traeger grabbed the rag that sat on his bike seat. "Hopefully, she won't wake up and freak because she doesn't know where she is."

"I'm planning on going up and leaving my door open."

"You're not going to crash with her?" Trager asked, surprised.

"As much as I want to, I don't want to fuck this up."

Traeger nodded as he polished the chrome on his bike.

"When are you planning on moving into your room?"

He shrugged. As long as he had a place to crash, he was fine. The fact that his old room was in the old part of the building put space between him and Tara, for when she got there. He still needed time to get his head out of his ass. "It doesn't matter to me. If she needs it, let her have it."

"It shouldn't be too long."

"You hope." Traeger chuckled.

"Fuck off. I'm also putting Tara in there. They'll share until we figure things out."

Traeger turned away. He didn't know how he felt about Tara living here at the club full-time. He'd have to see her every day, and if he decided he didn't want her, he'd have to watch one of his brothers have her.

"Are you pissed that she's coming, too?"

"No. Not at all," Traeger answered calmly. Frankly, he didn't know how he felt or what he was going to do.

"What do you want me to tell the guys? Is she up for grabs?"

Traeger felt his stomach twist into a knot at the thought, but Paula, his dead girlfriend, kept invading his mind.

"Sure. I'm not ready for a full-time woman."

"Jesus, it wasn't your fault. When are you going to get over it?" Fury spat out.

White-hot anger raced through Traeger as he stood and faced Fury. He'd been incredibly close to going for his prez, and that would have ended badly.

"Just shut the fuck up about it," he said and walked away.

"Fine, you stupid fuck. The guys will be thrilled at a chance at her."

He didn't know which was worse. The guilt he had because of his girlfriend's death or the anger at the thought of another man touching Tara.

Traeger ignored him and organized the tools on the far bench. He stayed that way until he heard Fury walk away.

A few hours later, he dragged himself to his bedroom, showered, and then dropped into bed. He had hoped that if he was tired enough, he'd be able to fall asleep without the guilt.

He was floored when it wasn't his girlfriend, Paula's face he saw like always in his dreams, but Tara's.

He didn't know what it meant or if it was good or bad, but he rested easier thinking about the little, sweet woman than he ever had thinking about Paula.

He'd only been asleep a few hours when he was jerked awake by Fury yelling for him and several men to ride. They were going to pick Tara up, and he still didn't know how he felt about it.

Chapter Four

Before six the next morning, Tara was dragged out of bed by someone pounding on her front door.

She pulled on her robe and walked to the door. "Who is it?"

"Fury."

She frowned.

"Tara, open the door."

She exhaled, unlocked, and opened the door a bit to talk to him. "Amelia doesn't live here."

She gasped, then he started pushing the door open.

"I know." He stepped in, moving her back in the process, and looked around.

"What are you doing here so early in the morning?"

Fury turned toward her. "Well, you see, Amelia has moved into the clubhouse, and she wants you there."

Her mouth dropped open. "Wait, what?"

"You heard me."

A suspicious thought entered her mind. "Did you give her a choice?"

He snorted. "Of course, I did. I'm not a kidnapper. At least most of the time."

Her eyes narrowed on the smirk on the guy's face.

"So, what am I supposed to do?" she asked.

"You're going to quit your job and move in and take care of us. We desperately need you two."

She crossed her arms over her chest. "Wait. Why? Like right now?" She didn't trust that smile on his face.

"Hell, yes, right now. I'll tell you what I did Amelia. We need you guys because we have two guys that can cook, and that's barely. We're all sick of the same shit or calling for takeout."

"How do you know I can cook?" she asked him suspiciously.

"Amelia told me."

"Oh."

She looked down and rubbed her eyes. The night had been especially hard. She'd awoken a few hours after getting home from the strip joint to find a few cop cars, Mrs. Clark, and an ambulance.

She'd asked the first person she caught what was happening.

It seemed her mother had gotten out of the apartment despite the different locks and furniture Tara used to prevent it. Fortunately, her mother had been in her nightgown, and it had been warm. The police called an ambulance when they found her because they hadn't known where her mother came from or her address. The ambulance had been there before and the paramedics knew her mom.

The group discussed the situation with her doctor over the phone, and it was determined that her mom should move into the specialized home that night instead of waiting for a few more weeks like they first had talked about. When she had tried to explain it to her mother, who was lying in the ambulance, she'd gotten even more agitated, so they had sedated her and driven her over to the home where she would live until she died.

Tara was trying to figure out how to get to the home to help her mother because buses weren't on the streets early.

They had called her and told her to give them at least a few days to get her settled. It might take longer before they thought it best that she would visit because it would upset her mother more. Then they explained that she should call the desk before making the trip to the residents' house. So, she had to call to get her information about how her mother was doing from a nurse for the next few weeks.

When Tara had climbed into bed, she'd had so many mixed feelings. She was glad that her mother was getting the help she needed and that some of the pressure was taken off of her, but then she also felt guilty she felt that way and knew she'd miss her mother terribly.

She'd been so exhausted nothing could keep her awake.

Now she had to deal with Fury.

"Listen, Fury, I'm really tired. So could you maybe come back later?"

He shook his head. "No. I want you to come with me now."

"Like right now? This is crazy."

"Amelia needs you there."

That made her pause.

"We're paying you more than you make here, and you won't have to spend money on rent."

Damn, that sounded good. She wanted to be able to keep her mother in the home they'd taken her to.

"So, I have to come with you right now? When will I be able to come back and get my stuff?"

"I have guys here to help pack it up."

"Like right now?"

"You keep saying that," Fury murmured impatiently.

"Well, I'm sorry. This is something I've never had to deal with before."

"Do what I say, and everything will be okay."

"Do I have a choice?"

He grinned and shrugged.

She jumped when he whistled, and then over a dozen guys walked in with boxes. She turned back to

Fury and saw Traeger had come in and was standing beside him, staring at her.

She tightened the belt on her robe. "I guess I'll go get dressed."

Fury snorted. "You better hurry because the guys are coming in and packing it up."

Tara pulled her attention from Traeger and jerked her gaze back to Fury. "Now, wait…"

Fury ignored her and looked at Traeger. "Can you get her moving? I don't have all day."

She saw the anger fill Traeger's eyes and wondered about it. She figured he didn't want to have to deal with her. "I don't need help."

They both ignored her.

"Hey, I'm sorry I asked," he said to Traeger and then turned around. "Rage, I need you to help Tara get a move on…"

"Fuck that," Traeger said with a growl as he grabbed her upper arm and moved her toward the bedroom.

"Wait, what are you doing?" She ran to keep up with his steps.

Traeger grunted, got her into the bedroom, and shut the door, then leaned against it.

"Get some clothes on, babe. Unless you want me to take you out of here in that?"

She gritted her teeth at his snide tone and the eyebrow he raised at her.

"Well, babe," she said back, almost smiling at the surprise on his face. "I'm a big girl now. So I don't need my daddy to help me dress."

Traeger straightened. The intense look he gave her made her nervous, so she walked over to her dresser and pulled out some clothes.

"You can leave now. As you can see, I'm getting

dressed."

He crossed his arms over his chest. "No, I'll stay."

She wanted to wipe the smirk off his face but decided she'd shock him instead. She ripped her robe off her shoulders and threw it on the bed before tugging the nightgown over her head.

Tara pulled on her clothes, watching the look in his eyes the whole time. She loved how shocked he was. He really hadn't expected her to do something like that, she thought.

She sat on the bed, pulled on socks and then her shoes. Then she stood in front of him and held her arms out.

"How'd I do, daddy?" she asked sarcastically.

She squeaked when he reached for her and held her on to her shoulders, pushing her onto her tiptoes in front of him. She was amazed how fast the big guy could move.

"You like pushing me, babe?"

She swallowed. "No, babe, but I'm not taking your shit either."

God, what had gotten into her? She had to admit she like the heat and passion on his face better than the cold eyes and indifference.

He grabbed a chunk of her hair and tipped her head back. His gaze traced over her features for a long moment, slowly driving her crazy.

She was disappointed when instead of kissing her like she thought he would do, he set her away from him, turned, and walked out of the bedroom.

When a few guys with boxes walked in, she was pulled from her daze as they set them on the bed and started dumping everything in them.

"Jeez, guys," she said and pushed one of them out of the way. She and the two men packed up her bedroom and her mother's in less than thirty minutes.

By the time she walked into the living room, everything else was packed, and they'd taken some boxes out already.

Holy cow. These guys moved fast.

"Can the furniture stay?" Fury asked.

She shrugged. It was old and worn. She hadn't wanted to spend any money on stuff like that. "Sure."

"Good, let's go then."

She looked around one more time and silently said goodbye to another chapter of her life.

Chapter Five

Fury glanced her way and then pointed to a guy a few feet away. "You're going to ride with him."

Her eyes widened. "On the back of his bike?"

"Yeah. Is there a problem with that?"

She sighed. "No." She looked at the guy. "What's your name?"

"Enforcer."

She just nodded, too tired to ask him questions.

Enforcer waited patiently by the curb and helped her onto the back of his bike.

"I've never ridden on a bike before," she admitted to him.

Enforcer chuckled. "Holy fuck, a bike virgin?"

She snorted and then laughed.

"Wrap your arms around my waist, babe, and hold on tight."

She did and then squealed when he took off. "Oh, my God, this is fun," she yelled, making Enforcer laugh.

Tara noticed Traeger on another bike riding beside and a little behind them, but she ignored him the best she could. She did see the anger, and what she thought was jealousy he tried to hide from her.

She didn't know what his problem was, and although she found him incredibly handsome, she wasn't going to chase a man who didn't want her. Instead, she decided she'd concentrate on her new life with the bikers, her friend Amelia, and her mother.

That was enough for her.

****

Traeger couldn't pull his eyes off the woman riding on the bike in front of him. Her long soft hair streamed out behind her, and he could hear the joy in her laughter. Something he couldn't remember hearing before in his life.

He'd grown up with his deadbeat mom. His focus had been staying alive, so he could get himself out of the dump they lived in. When he was seventeen, he'd met Fury, and they'd decided to build their own biker club. Fury had come from the lifestyle. His father had been the prez of his club, and his older brother was destined to take over, leaving Fury to stay in the background.

Fury hadn't been good with that, so he'd left, moved south, and started his own club. Several guys had come with him when he left his home and a few he'd picked up along the way.

Traeger had won the right to be by his side as his vice prez when he'd saved Fury's life not once, but twice, and was able to beat down any of the guys. He'd fallen into the position like he was made for it. Their club grew quickly and got the reputation of being brutal but only to the ones that crossed them. Civilians were in no danger from them, and actually, they'd come to accept the club's protection over the years.

Now he was lusting after a woman who didn't belong in his life, and he didn't think she'd fit in with the club. Tara was too sweet and innocent.

Although the shit she pulled back in her bedroom had thrown him for a loop. It was the last thing he'd expected the timid woman to do. But then she was turning out not to be what he thought in the beginning.

The fact she was riding with one of his brothers and laughing made him angry at himself that he hadn't grabbed her when he had the chance.

At the club, the guys parked, and Enforcer got off his bike and helped Tara off. She groaned and clutched at the arms around her when her legs gave out.

Enforcer was saying something to her as she

laughed.

Traeger thought his head was about ready to blow when he walked up to them, pushed Enforcer aside, and lifted her in his arms.

"Why'd you do that?" she asked as she wrapped her arms around his neck.

"Because I wanted to."

"Do you always get what you want?"

He chuckled at the disgust in her tone. "Yeah."

"Well, don't become too used to it because it will suck when it fails, and it usually does at some point," she said snidely.

He could guess what she was referring to. Him wanting her, and he grinned. "We'll see about that."

She nodded. "Yes, we will."

He took her into the kitchen and set her on her feet. He held her tight to make sure she was steady before he took a step back.

"Go ahead and get acquainted with the kitchen. The guys will bring your things up to the room when you're ready."

"That's fine."

He nodded, turned, and left. Once outside, he leaned against the club and wiped a hand down his face. How the fuck was he going to deal with being around Tara all the time and not grabbing her?

He knew he would claim her because the thought of one of his brothers touching her, feeling her tight cunt and full breasts, made him murderous.

It wasn't going to happen.

Now he had to figure out how to deal with the residual guilt he felt because of Paula's death. He knew he hadn't been the one to pull the trigger that took her life, but his actions against the man who did were what caused the guy to go after his woman.

What made it so much worse was that he'd been right beside her and hadn't protected her.

They'd just been walking along the street when she'd been shot. The guy, Mathews, had driven up beside them in a car, drew a gun, and before Traeger could get to him or protect her, Matthews had pulled the trigger, ending her life right before Traeger's eyes.

The bastard had run then. It had taken Traeger a few months to find him, but when he did, he'd made the fucker pay severely. He kept him alive for five days, slowly taking parts of him making the guy scream before he'd finally died.

Traeger had been furious that it had ended so quickly, and it took Fury and several other brothers to pull him away from the corpse.

He'd taken off on his bike and hadn't come back for seven months, trying to burn some of the hatred out of him so he didn't take off on one of the brothers. He'd been very close to losing it.

When he did show, Fury walked up to him, hugged him, and welcomed him home. The whole club had been glad to have him back. They'd partied for three days straight, and Traeger had fucked every whore they had a few times before he finally calmed enough to start living again.

What got to him at that moment was that he hadn't been living so much as existing. He hadn't let Paula go yet. It had been four years, and he still hadn't let himself free of the guilt. It was holding him back.

Until Tara came into his life—she unknowingly brought him back to the living. Giving him hope that he could have a relationship again. He'd do things a little differently this time. He'd have her protected the whole time. She wouldn't leave the compound with less than two guys.

Now, he had to make himself take the second step, which would be the hardest of all. The first was admitting and forgiving himself, and the next was to claim her as his own.

He exhaled. Fuck, yeah. This might be harder than he first thought, but he knew he couldn't let her go. No matter what.

Chapter Six

Tara was stirring the eggs in the pan when the door burst open and Amelia raced through.

She burst out a laugh and ran to her. They ignored the men staring at them and hugged for a long time until they both smelled something burning and raced to the stove.

She was thankful the eggs were saved because she didn't really want to start all over again.

Tara smiled at the shock on Amelia's face at the size of the pan. It was easily bigger than four pans put together. It was lightweight, but she would still need help to move it when it was full.

"How many eggs do you have in that pan?"

Tara chuckled. "Four dozen."

"Well, I would say that's too much, but with the group of men here and all of them oversized, we might just run out."

Amelia stood beside her and looked around.

Tara knew she was looking at a very large, beautiful kitchen. It was the nicest Tara had ever seen.

"What can I do while we talk?"

"Toast." Tara showed her where to put the food to keep warm.

"So, tell me how you got here? I was planning on calling you this morning and asking you if you'd like to be here with me."

Tara snorted and finished the eggs and set them in the warmer. "I certainly wasn't asked in a normal way."

She still couldn't believe she was standing in a motorcycle club's kitchen making them breakfast. Hell, maybe she was just dreaming? She shook her head.

"I recognized Fury from Dick's Place, so I opened the door."

"Oh, Lord. What happened?"

"He stepped into my apartment and told me you were living and working here and that you wanted me to come with you."

Tara chuckled. "I asked a bunch of questions before I finally agreed."

"Not two minutes after that, several men walked into my place and started packing everything. I just stood there with my mouth open until Fury barked at me to tell them what was going."

Amelia started laughing.

"I got to ride a motorcycle here."

"Oh, wow. How was it?"

"It was so much fun. I want to do it again. But anyway, we got me packed and was back here, and I was cooking."

Tara grinned when she noticed twelve guys stood there watching them. They all gazed at the women with heated looks, but she could also tell they were hungry for more than just them—namely the food they were making.

"Hey, guys, it's not quite done. We can yell when it is," Amelia said.

"That's okay. We'll wait."

Tara jumped and almost peed her pants when Fury yelled at the men.

"We're just watching, boss."

"Do you guys mind if you're gawked at?" Fury asked them.

She and Tara shrugged.

"Not as long as they stay out of the way," Amelia said.

Tara grinned when Fury walked up behind Amelia. They whispered for a moment.

Fury walked out, telling them they could throw something at the men if they got crazy.

"We will. Thank you for bringing Tara here."

"You can thank me later," he told Amelia.

"What does that mean?" Amelia asked, seeming confused.

It made Tara giggle before she called out. "Bacon is about done."

They set everything out on the counter, and Tara watched in amazement as the food dwindled rather quickly, but at least they thought most all of them had gone through.

"We better scramble some more eggs." Amelia started cracking them into a bowl while Tara heated the pan.

After filling the bowl, the woman leaned against the counter, drank coffee, and watched the men when Fury and Traeger came into the kitchen.

That man was dangerous to her heart. Tara tried to ignore Traeger the best she could, but the man seemed to suck the air from the room.

"Here you go," Amelia told Fury when she handed him a plate of food. "Tara and I will figure out how much you all eat."

Fury snorted. "It wouldn't matter. They keep eating until it's gone. Just do the best you can. It's a hell of a lot more than they were getting."

Tara watched as they walked out of the room, talking with their plates in their hands.

Her heart tripped in her chest when she caught sight of Traeger's ass. He filled out the jeans he wore well. Oh, Lord, she really had the hots for the guy. It was so stupid since he mostly just glared at her.

Tara started wiping down the counter. She knew she had to tell Amelia everything about the night before, and she might be hurt because she'd led her to believe her mom was already in the home.

"Hey, my mom was taken to the home last night. I was woken up about three this morning and found her outside in an ambulance. She'd gotten out of the house and was walking around outside in her nightgown."

"Oh, my God. Is she okay?"

"Yes."

Tara saw the confusion in Amelia's eyes and felt terrible.

"It sounded like she was already there," Amelia said in confusion.

"I'm sorry. I didn't want to talk about it. It was consuming my life, and I needed a break."

"Yeah. I understand that." Amelia hugged her.

Tara wiped a tear from her eye. "I hate to say that I'm glad it happened."

"I understand that, too. You kept her with you longer than most everyone would have."

"Am I always going to feel like it wasn't enough?"

"Yeah. But it gets easier. I promise."

Tara hugged her again before she and Amelia grabbed the bowls and put them to soak in the sink as they wiped up the kitchen.

Tara's head jerked up as five scantily-clad women stumbled into the kitchen.

"Where the fuck is the food?" one of them yelled.

Tara's mouth fell open.

Amelia cleared her throat. "I'm sorry, but it's gone."

"Then make us some more," a thin fake redhead demanded.

Tara started to tell the woman to fuck off and got interrupted.

"That's not going to fucking happen."

Everyone turned toward the door.

"If you whores can't get up at a reasonable time, you feed yourselves," Traeger said with a growl.

"That's not fucking fair."

Amelia and Tara glanced at each other as Traeger stalked toward the woman.

Tara covered her mouth when he took a chunk of the mouthy one's hair and got in her face. "You don't fucking get it, whore. You're here for one reason, and that's a hole for the boys to fuck. Maybe if you'd get off your scrawny asses and helped around here, I'd go easier on you, but all you do is sit around or fuck. No one would think twice about you if you disappeared, so watch yourself."

He yanked her head away from him, making her cry out in pain, and walked out.

Tara was shocked at the cruelty of the man she'd become attracted to. It should have taken away from how much she wanted him, but the fact he was sticking up for her and Amelia, and she didn't like the women at all, made her attraction deepen.

She didn't know if that was wrong, but she couldn't help her feelings.

Tara was surprised when the mouthy one turned back to them, angry.

"You fucking skanks, you're here to be maids and nothing else. So stay the fuck away from the guys. It's not like they're going to like your fat asses, anyway."

The group turned and walked out.

Tara exhaled to steady her heart as it tried to pulse out of her chest.

She saw the fear in Amelia's eyes.

"That was intense."

"Ya think?" she said and laughed.

"Let's go back to the list of meals. Then I think we should set up a menu plan for the whole week and make a grocery list. What do you think?" Amelia asked.

Tara nodded and then yawned.

"Are you doing okay?" Amelia asked her. "You need to nap. You haven't gotten a lot of sleep for a long time."

She shook her head. "No. I want to help with this and then call the care facility and see about Mom."

"All right, but if I can do anything, please tell me."

The pantry was in such disarray, it took them a lot longer than they anticipated. There was no organization, and it hadn't been cleaned in months.

Amelia touched her hand. "God, I'm glad Fury let you come with me. I could never have done this by myself very easily."

Tara grinned. "I'm glad, too. Although I never saw myself living with a motorcycle gang, you're the only person besides my mom I care about." God, if her mother could see her now.

"I feel the same about you. I consider you my sister."

"Ditto." Tara fist-bumped her.

"Hell, we better get lunch going."

Tara glanced at the clock. "I didn't realize it was so late. But I suspect they'll still be thrilled with it no matter what time we put it out."

"You're right about that."

Chapter Seven

Tara and Amelia finished putting everything out for lunch.

She leaned back against the cabinet and tightened her ponytail that had come loose when the women from the morning came in. Without a word, they grabbed a bunch of the food, filling their plates to the brim, and walked out, smiling at them.

Amelia glanced at Tara, and she just shrugged.

She didn't know if she'd be able to deal with these bitches every day.

A stream of guys came through at a steady pace, and Tara saw the food start to dwindle quickly. She thought about the woman who had come through. If they thought taking all the food was hurting them in any way, they were wrong. It would end up hurting the guys if they ran out before everyone ate.

Amelia looked at her. "I think we should make Fury and Traeger a plate again before it's all gone."

"Good idea." Tara nodded.

"While the club is getting their food, let's start on dinner."

"We have the fixings for chili and cornbread," Tara said. She actually made delicious chili and was now craving it. It had been a while since she had made it because her mother hadn't been able to eat things like it.

"I don't have half the spices I need for it, but it should taste fine," Amelia said.

Tara nodded. There were a dozen or more spices they needed. "But we need to make a list of the ones we need."

"The chili won't be award-winning, but it will taste good enough."

Fury and Traeger came in for their food. Tara smiled as Fury had his hands all over Amelia. They really did look good together. She would never have thought that until she saw them just then.

"Hey, how's the day going so far?"

Tara turned to answer Traeger. She was shocked he was talking to her. "Good."

"If you need any help to settle in, just let me know."

She nodded. "There is one thing. My mom is in a care facility for Alzheimer's patients."

"I'm sorry to hear that."

Tara nodded, looked away, and swallowed to prevent herself from crying. "Anyway. I'll be able to go see her in a week or so, and I might need to leave for the afternoon. I'm not sure how long it will take to get there from here on the bus…"

"You're not riding the fucking bus, babe. Just tell me when and I'll take you."

"You don't have to do that."

He cupped her chin. "Let me put it this way. You leave the compound without me or at least one of the other guys I assign to you, and you'll be in deep shit."

Her eyes narrowed. "I didn't know I was going to be a prisoner…"

He scowled. "Fuck that. You're not. I'm going to want you protected at all times. You can go wherever you want, but with one of us. Is that too much to ask?"

She sighed. "No, I guess not. I just hate bothering you guys for something like this."

He swept his thumb over her cheek, making her shiver. "You're not."

"Okay."

The back door slammed, catching all their attention. The whores who walked in froze at the sight of the Fury and Traeger.

Tara saw the men look at the women's plates and knew by the way the men stiffened they were in deep shit.

"You're eating all of that. If you put it on your plate, it won't go to waste," Fury said with a growl. Then he yelled, "Enforcer!"

Enforcer came through the door. "Yeah, boss."

"Take the woman into the living area, and I want you to watch them eat every fucking bite on their plates. I don't care if they puke. They keep eating."

Tara leaned back against the counter as Fury dealt with the whores.

"They filled their plates for what purpose?"

Tara shrugged. "We don't know."

"I think they were trying to piss you off or get back at you from this morning," Traeger guessed with a raised brow.

"What happened this morning?" Fury asked.

Traeger told him how the women had come in and yelled for food, but everything had already been put away. He said that he stepped in, but it must not have gotten through them about the disrespect.

Tara was afraid of the look that came into the man's eyes.

"Get Tara and follow."

Traeger pulled her out into the main room, over to where the whores were sitting, already looking like they were going to puke. She almost felt sorry for them.

"Listen up, you fucking cunts," Fury said.

Tara flinched. She wasn't used to being around that type of language. Even at the strip joint, the woman hadn't talked like this.

"These two women are under my protection. If I hear of any of you disrespect them like I heard you did this morning, I'll have a few of the guys take you out, beat you, and bury you."

Tara watched the color drain from the women's faces.

"Do you understand what I'm saying? I'm almost tempted to throw your skanky asses out. I think the boys would like some new meat."

"We'll be good, Fury," one of them said hurriedly.

Tara followed Traeger, Amelia, and Fury back into the kitchen. She giggled when Fury pressed Amelia against the wall.

"Hey," Traeger said to get her attention. "I'll be out back if you need me."

"Okay. Thank you." Tara watched him go out the door before she turned around and started stirring the chili.

A loud sound from the other room made her jump.

"Hey, boss, can you come here?" someone yelled from the living room.

"Jesus Christ, it's like running a preschool. I'll be seeing you later, babe," Fury told Amelia.

Tara bit her lip to keep from laughing at the disgust in his tone.

The rest of the afternoon, the girls made lists of what inventory they had and what they needed. Amelia showed Tara the room they were staying in and helped her get the stuff she'd need, like her bathroom things and clothes.

Tara looked longingly at the bed and told herself she'd be in it in a few short hours where she might get the best night of sleep she'd had in months.

The guys loved the chili they served that night, and both women were thrilled they'd made enough for everyone to get their fill.

When the club whores came through the line, they ignored Amelia and her, which was fine, and they took very little food with them and returned to the main room.

"Come on outside, girls, you've spent all day in here," Fury yelled.

Tara wiped her hands. She was looking forward to sitting outside and relaxing. The moment she was out the door, one of the men picked her up. She didn't know which one it was. He laughed when she screamed and then threw her in the pool.

She came up sputtering with her long hair hanging in her face. "Are you kidding me, you jerk?" Tara yelled, making the guys sitting around the backyard laugh.

Tara pulled herself from the pool and wrung her shirt and then her hair out, glaring at all of them.

"God, what if I couldn't swim?" she asked them.

The one she thought was Burn chuckled. "That's why I was standing here, babe. Just in case."

She rolled her eyes. "Wow, how gallant of you."

The guys threw back their heads and laughed loudly. She sniffed in disgust and walked into the house. She left wet footprints in a trail through the kitchen, up the stairs, and to the bedroom Amelia had shown her before.

After a nice hot shower and drying her hair, she pulled on a nightgown and panties and crawled into bed. Between one minute and the next, she was out.

She had no idea how much time passed when she was aware of Amelia coming into the room and going to the bathroom. Tara must have gone back to sleep because she awoke again when Amelia crawled into bed beside her and pulled the blanket up.

"How much longer do you think you can hold out with Fury?" Tara asked in a groggy tone.

"As long as I can."

Tara snorted. She waited for a moment. "I like it here. I feel safe, which is ridiculous because I know they're a vicious motorcycle club, but I don't think the men would ever harm us."

"I know they won't. I know what you mean. I don't remember ever feeling this relaxed or anxious for the next day to see what happens. Before we came here, I dreaded having to get out of bed."

Tara agreed.

"Do you like Traeger, Tara?"

"Yeah, but I'm not sure he likes me. I catch him staring at me, but then he ignores me when we run into each other."

"I've seen him stare at you when you're not looking. I can guarantee he's hot for you."

"We'll see," Tara said. "We just moved in, and I don't want to rock the boat. I feel like we already made some enemies with the women."

Amelia sighed. "Yeah, I agree. We'll just have to watch each other's backs."

"That's easy. We already do that."

"You're right about that."

"Night."

"Night, Tara."

****

The bedroom door opened an hour later.

Fury and Traeger stood staring at the women as they talked about a problem with shipments being stolen.

"God, I want that woman so bad I ache."

Traeger grinned and knew how Fury was feeling. "Then take her. You know she won't be able to resist you."

"I'm going to shower, and then I'll come back for her."

"I'll wait."

Fury glanced at him. "You're going to stay with Tara?"

Traeger thought back to earlier in the day when a few of the guys asked Fury about Tara and if she was available. He heard Fury tell them yeah, but to treat her like a lady and not a whore.

He'd been shocked at the rage that had gone through him at the thought of some other man touching her.

Since the moment he saw her, he'd decided she'd been his. He knew he was trying to fight it, but he also knew he was losing that fight. He hadn't declared her his yet, but it would happen soon.

"Yeah. I just want to hold her. I haven't held a woman for a long time."

Fury slapped his shoulder. "I think you two would be good for each other."

"We'll see. I'm not sure I can move forward yet, but my hands are itching worse than I can ever remember."

"I'm glad to hear it. I'll be right back."

Traeger relaxed against the dresser, crossed his arms, and stared at Tara.

She looked so peaceful and innocent. It should have turned him off because he'd always been more comfortable with women with experience, who knew the score and were rough around the edges. Instead, with this woman, his protective instincts came out with a vengeance. It kind of shocked him how strong his feelings were for this woman he'd known for only a short while.

Traeger was still leaning against the dresser with his gaze on the bed when Fury came back.

"I'll get Amelia out of here."

Fury reached over Tara and picked Amelia up.

"Night."

"Night," Traeger said before he closed and locked the door. He stripped, showered, and slid naked into bed beside Tara. He carefully pulled her back against his chest and then wrapped an arm around her waist.

He was amazed at how deeply she slept, but then he remembered she'd had to take care of her mother, and they'd woken her up very early. He was surprised she was able to function as well as she did all day without a nap.

Traeger exhaled and felt the tension slip away. He stuck his nose in her hair and inhaled. His cock had been semi-hard too hard since he'd met her, but now it was at an aching rigidness that made him groan because there was nothing he could do about it.

She mumbled something in her sleep and then pushed her ass against his groin.

"Shit," he hissed under his breath. He started a list of things he needed to get done the next day, trying to get his mind off his aching body. Nothing helped, but he wasn't going to leave her. She felt so good in his arms. He couldn't remember Paula feeling this good, and then guilt hit him. He should never compare the two because they were so different, but he couldn't help it.

Paula had grown up around bikers. Tattoos had covered her chest and arms and some of her back and legs. She also had several piercings, something he couldn't see Tara do.

He hadn't seen her body, but he would guess she didn't have any tattoos either. She was coming to him innocent and as unspoiled as a woman could get, and she could be all his if he got his head out of his ass long enough to claim her.

Every minute that went by made him more anxious to claim her, and he knew it wouldn't be long because he couldn't hold out much longer. He tightened his arm around her, closed his eyes, and fell to sleep.

At different times during the night, he'd wake up when she tried to move away from him and pull her back where she belonged.

Chapter Eight

Tara sighed, and her eyes fluttered open. God, she was still tired, but nothing like she had been before.

She stretched and then gasped when the weight around her waist moved. Her head jerked around to see Traeger asleep.

He growled when she tried to move away.

"Traeger," she whispered.

"Hmmm?"

"What are you doing in my bed?"

He opened one eye. "Technically, it's my bed."

"Well, no one told me that. If you let me go, I'll get up."

He closed his eyes. "No."

A frown puckered her brows. "What do you mean *no*?"

"Babe, go back to sleep."

"No. I need to get up."

"No, you don't. It's only five in the morning."

"I mean, I have to use the restroom." She felt herself blush.

He smirked. "You were stripping, and you're embarrassed to talk about peeing?"

She tried to push him away. "I have to go."

"If I let you up, you better come right back."

"But I'm not used to … you know … being in bed with a man."

"That's good to know because I'm the only man you're going to be in bed with from now on."

"You can't say stuff like that."

"I just did. Now go."

She slipped out of bed and rushed into the bathroom. After using the toilet and washing her hands, she brushed her teeth. She looked down at herself. She was wearing a nightgown that covered her from her shoulders to an inch above her knees, but it was white with little blue flowers. The material was thin enough she could see her tight nipples poking out.

It was a little better if she kept the front away from her body. He would still be able to see the shadows, but she could live with that.

She stood by the door with her hand on the doorknob. What would happen if she got dressed and left?

"I know what you're thinking, babe. If I were you, I wouldn't test me. Get your ass back here."

She sighed and opened the door.

Oh, Lord. He was raised up on one elbow, facing the bathroom door. The sight of his bare chest caught her attention and made her freeze. She'd known he was built by the way his t-shirts fit, but naked, he seemed even bigger, even more formidable.

"Come here."

She swallowed and walked to the bed. He flipped the blanket back.

"Get in."

When she didn't move fast enough, he reached out, grabbed her hand, and pulled her toward him.

She tried to resist, but he was too strong.

He maneuvered her until her back was against his chest again, and he tucked the blanket around them.

She stiffened. "Um, hey, Traeger. You're not…"

"Not what?"

"Um, naked?"

He chuckled. "Um, yeah, I am."

"Like right now?" she squeaked.

He laughed. "Yeah."

"Why?"

"I always sleep naked. You'll get used to it."

She shook her head. "No, I don't think so." The sense of power and danger in his large body took her breath. Instead of scaring her off, she went closer like a moth to a flame. Like it was inevitable, and there was nothing she could do to fight it.

"I do. Now go to sleep. If we keep talking, I'm going to pull you under me."

"Wait…"

"No. This is your last chance."

She pressed her lips together. She knew he wasn't the type of man to say things he didn't mean, so she kept quiet.

She heard his breathing deepen and didn't think she'd be able to sleep, but the next thing she knew, it was nine o'clock. She tried to scramble out of bed.

She gasped. "Oh, no, Amelia is probably already in the kitchen."

He tightened his arm and then threw his leg over her hips. "I sincerely doubt it. I'd bet Fury was at her all night, and she's tired."

"I … oh." Her eyes slid closed, and a shiver raced down her spine when she felt his teeth and lips on her neck and shoulder.

She twisted her head to the side to give him better access to her.

"Fuck, you smell and taste good," he murmured.

Air stuck in her throat when she felt his cock throb against her ass.

"Oh," she gasped when one of his large hands covered her breast.

"Jesus, you're so fucking juicy, babe."

"I … I don't know what to do."

"With what?" he mumbled against her neck.

"I don't know if I'm ready for where this is

going."

He nodded but didn't stop caressing her breast and nibbling on her shoulder.

"I get it. I just want to touch you right now. Will you let me play for a bit?"

"I … um … okay."

He chuckled. "I'm just going to make you feel good."

"Can I make you feel good, too?"

"Later."

He rolled her onto her back, cupped her face with his hand, lowered his head, and took her mouth with a hunger that made her hot but scared her with its intensity.

"Easy," he said. "I just want to show you I can give you. I can make you feel so fucking good." His lips slid down and captured one of her tits.

She whimpered when he sucked it in and then tongued it against the roof of his mouth. She could feel his actions through the thin fabric of her nightgown.

She arched off the mattress and slid her fingers into his thick hair to hold him tightly against her.

He lifted his head and chuckled. "I'll give you more." His hand slid down her torso and then dipped into her panties.

She crossed her legs to keep him from between her thighs.

He laughed. "Let me in."

"No."

"But I can make you feel good."

"I'm sure you can. You've probably fucked hundreds of girls."

He snorted. "I don't think that many, but hey, just think. My experience is in your favor because I know how to make you come in numerous different ways."

He was finally able to get one finger to delve in

between her pussy lips and press on her clit.

"Ahh," she cried, and her legs fell open.

He grinned as he slid his finger up into her cunt. "Fucking H. Christ, you're so fucking tight. You're going to strangle my cock when I get it into you." He pulled out, added another, and forced them into her. "That's it, take them."

"It's too much," she whimpered.

"Babe, it's only two fingers. My cock is a hell of a lot bigger than this."

"I won't be able to do it."

"Fuck yeah, you will." He finger fucked her for a few moments. "I can't wait to try your ass."

"Wait…"

"You've never had someone up your ass?"

"No, never."

"How many men have you been with?"

"Just one."

"How long ago?"

"I don't know, four or five years." She could feel a flush of embarrassment. "I don't have a lot of experience."

Chapter Nine

He couldn't believe his ears.

"Jesus, have you given a blowjob before?"

She shook her head.

She's practically a virgin, he thought as he pumped his fingers into her tight sheath. He'd be the only man to have her. No other man would ever touch her. No more whore pussy for him. The wave of possessiveness that filled him shocked him. He wanted to protect her from everything and teach her all the things he liked. He'd make sure she'd never say no to him.

He'd never felt this way about Paula. That made guilt show its ugly head, but he pushed it down. They were two different women in about every way imaginable.

Paula had been tall and skinny. She'd lost her virginity at thirteen and been hard and distrustful and found fault with just about everything.

Tara was small and curvy and so damn sweet it made his teeth ache. There wasn't a hard bone in her body. He'd never thought he'd feel less than anyone, but knowing she was his, he silently wondered if he was good enough for her. Even though he thought that way, there was no way in hell he'd let her go or allow another man to touch her. She was his, and she better come to grips with it.

"You're fucking mine." He stared down at her as she writhed against him while he continued to finger fuck her hard and fast.

He'd never seen anything this fucking beautiful in his life.

Traeger cradled her against his chest and held her steady for his loving. He tipped her head with a hand supporting the back of her head and took her lips. He bit her bottom lip and then moved down to her neck and then her shoulder, where he bit down hard enough that he'd see it for the rest of the day.

"I want you to come for me."

She shook her head. "No." She was shaking but fighting the pleasure he was giving her.

"You'll come for me now, or I'll keep up the torment until you do. Nothing's going to happen to you. I won't let it. Now … come."

The scream that tore from her throat was pure music to his ears and had him coming from the sound, the smell of her arousal, and the tight clasp her cunt had on his fingers.

He pulled as much pleasure out of her as he could, prolonging it as long as he could because he was enthralled with the picture she made.

Only when she collapsed against him did he stop forcing his way into her. He kept his fingers inside of her for a long moment because it was the best feeling in the world, and he didn't want it to end.

He couldn't imagine how it would feel on his cock, and he decided he just might die from the pleasure. Traeger pulled his fingers out of her and stuck them in his mouth, sucking off every little bit of her cum he could. It was a flavor he was already addicted to.

"What about you?" she murmured against his neck.

He grinned at her shyness.

"I came, babe."

She leaned away from him with wide eyes. "Really?"

"Yeah." He grinned. "I haven't done that since I was thirteen."

"Thirteen? You had sex when you were thirteen?"

He smoothed the hair away from her face. She looked so scandalized, it made him chuckle.

"Where I grew up, there wasn't a home life. It was survival of the fittest, so I grew up rather quickly."

Her fingertips touched his mouth, and the look of pure sadness for him made his stomach twist. Had he ever had someone care about him this much?

Oh, he knew Paula had cared, but it was a selfish kind of love. If she didn't get what she wanted from him, she could have easily walked away from him. His MC family also cared, but if he died, they'd mourn him for only so long and move on rather quickly because it was a part of their lives. They knew the danger they put themselves in. Their lifespans were shorter than an average man's, so it was just a part of life when one of them died.

He had a feeling if Tara fell in love with him, she'd mourn him for the rest of her life, and that kind of emotion scared him but at the same time humbled him. The men he lived with were considered family, but he and Tara would make their own little family that he didn't have to share.

"I'm so sorry. What about your parents?"

"I don't know who my father was. My mom was a prostitute so she could feed her drug addiction."

He saw the shock on her face and wondered if knowing where he'd come from would make her run from him.

"God, Traeger, I'm so sorry. Where is she now?"

He shrugged. He couldn't remember the last time he thought about her. "I have no idea. I left when I was a teenager and never looked back."

"A teenager? What did you do?"

"I met up with Fury, and we started the club."

"And now how old are you?"

"I'm thirty-six."

"Twelve years older than me."

One of his eyebrows rose. "Yeah, does that bother you?" he asked.

She shook her head. "No. I like that you're older. Maybe I could call you daddy."

He chuckled. "You're a smartass."

"Maybe."

"What about you?"

"It was just my mom and me. She and my dad adopted me when they were older. My dad died when I was three, so it was just the two of us for about twenty years. She worked two and three jobs to support us, and I took care of the house the best I could and had meals ready for her."

"How old were you?"

She smiled. "I'm not sure. I remember trying to sweep the floor, but the broom was twice my size. I also remember having to stand on a chair by the stove so I could reach to stir whatever I made."

"Are we talking eight or nine years old?"

She shook her head. "No, I was probably five."

"She left you alone when she worked?" God, the thought of all the things that could have happened to her made him sick.

"We lived in an apartment, and there was a nice neighbor who lived next door that I could go to if I needed anything. The whole building kind of looked out for me. It was too expensive to pay someone to babysit. I've always been responsible, so she never had to worry about me burning down the apartment."

"Still, I can't imagine you by yourself. You were just a baby."

"Weren't you left by yourself at times?"

He nodded. "Yeah, a lot."

"See, it happens."

"But I was never a baby."

"You were too."

"I don't ever remember feeling small or defenseless. I carried a knife with me since I was very young, and I used it a few times when guys my mom brought home would try to come at me."

He was shocked to see the tears that filled her eyes.

"Oh, my God, that's horrible. They would try to touch you?" she asked, outraged.

He used his thumb to wipe them away. He was as sure as he could be that no one had ever cried for him.

"Jesus. You're so fucking sweet."

She hugged him tightly but didn't say anything.

"Let's get up, babe. I know I have work to do, and you have food to make."

"Yes. I don't like leaving Amelia on her own. It's quite the job feeding you guys."

He was almost afraid to ask. "Do you enjoy it?"

She smiled. "Very much. I love cooking and taking care of people, and the fact you guys make me feel safe is huge to me."

"You are safe. Nothing is going to touch you here, but you'll have to listen to me at all times. If I find you disobeyed, you'll be punished."

He pulled the blanket back so she could slide out.

He watched her pull clothes on.

"So, you will be kind of like a daddy."

He smirked and then laughed when he stood. She squeaked when she caught sight of his naked body and twirled around so her back was to him.

"Oh, I'm going to be that and much more."He grabbed her shoulders and pressed up against her back. "I'm going to be your whole world."

She sucked in a startled breath.

"Can you handle that?" he asked.

"Um … yes. I think so."

"Good. Now go use the restroom." He smacked her ass to get her going. "I'll meet you downstairs."

He watched her scurry into the bathroom and close the door. He couldn't remember being this happy or looking forward to the future. Yeah, he was definitely keeping her.

Chapter Ten

Tara made it downstairs only to find Amelia had just arrived.

"Oh, wow. I thought I was late."

Amelia smiled at her over her shoulder as she pulled eggs from the refrigerator. "No. I just got down here."

Tara saw the blush that covered her friend's face and grinned. "Any reason you are blushing?"

Amelia scowled at her and started cracking eggs in a bowl.

"It's just I figured you were in Fury's bed when I woke up, and you weren't there this morning."

Amelia nodded. "Yes, I'm not sure what time he woke me up, but I ended up in his bed."

Tara knew from the look on her face they'd had sex. "Was it good?"

Amelia started cracking up. "Oh, God, yes. I never thought it could feel like that."

"What?"

"I don't know how to describe it other than to say it was amazing."

Tara's heart beat heavily in her chest. Trager just using his fingers on her had been fantastic. She didn't know if she'd be able to handle having his cock in her if it got better.

"I'm so happy for you." Tara hugged her and then pulled the bacon out.

Within thirty minutes, they were setting everything out, and guys were starting to come through.

"Jeez, they eat a lot."

"They're all so freaking big, they need all the calories," Tara guessed. "I'm going to get some of the things we'll need for lunch out of the pantry."

Amelia nodded and started making more toast.

They had decided on making soup for lunch, but she also wanted to make cookies, and she hoped they had everything they needed for them.

She stiffened when one arm came around her waist, and the other hand pressed over her mouth to keep her from screaming. Fear shot through her, and she started to struggle.

"Hey, easy, babe. It's just me. I'm sorry. I didn't mean to scare you."

She exhaled in relief when she heard Traeger's voice. She pulled his hand from her mouth. "Why are you creeping up on me?"

He chuckled. "I saw you come in here, and I thought it was a great opportunity to get my hands on you."

She gripped the shelf in front of her when one of his hands covered a breast and started squeezing and plucking at the nipple.

"Oh, God," she moaned and leaned against him.

He used his other hand to push her hair that she'd left loose out of his way before his nose ran up and down her neck. Then he started sucking on her.

From the slight pinch, she knew she'd have a mark when he was done, but at the moment, she didn't care. Her eyes slid closed, and she tilted her head a bit more, giving him more room.

"Jesus, woman. I need to fuck you soon before I go fucking crazy."

"Mmmm." The sensations running through her made it next to impossible to understand everything he was saying.

He pressed his cock against the small of her back and slid the hand that wasn't caressing her breast down her midsection, and then pressed against her clit over her jeans.

"Babe, I hate these jeans. I want you in skirts with no panties so I can get you to whenever I want."

"What? No panties? I can't do that."

He bit down on her neck at the same time he put pressure on her clit and tit. "You fucking will. You'll find out soon enough how serious I am. I dare you to push me."

She tried to pull herself out of the haze of desire he'd put her in. "Wait, you can't do that."

"Do you want to be mine? Do you want me to make you feel better than you ever had in your life?"

She was so confused. She wanted to yell yes, but the good girl inside of her questioned the fact they hardly knew each other. "I don't know…"

"Answer me this. Do you want me?"

She sighed and nodded. "Yes."

"And I want you, and that's all that matters. Babe, you make me feel things I've never felt before."

"Me, too."

"Good. Don't question it too much. You waste time with that shit. We're not hurting anyone, and we make each other happy. Let's concentrate on that."

"Okay." She hadn't realized his hands had stopped caressing her until then, and she wanted to beg for more.

He pushed against her clit a few more times and bit down on her neck. "We've got to get to work, but think about this. Remember my hands and how good I can make you feel."

She sighed and nodded. "Okay."

He pressed a kiss to the back of her head. "Good girl."

She clung to the shelf after he left as she waited

for the shaking in her limbs to cease. When she finally got the strength, she picked up the supplies she'd come in for and walked back into the kitchen.

A few of the guys were still going through getting their food.

The sudden quiet of the room seeped through her senses, and she turned to see everyone, including Amelia staring at her.

"What?" she asked as she wiped her face. "Do I have something on my face?"

They all laughed. The guys walked off, and Amelia came to stand next to her.

"Tell me," Tara said.

"It's just you walked into the pantry all buttoned up and calm, and you walked out with your hair tangled, her skin flush, and several hickeys on your neck."

She gasped and slapped a hand down on her neck. "Shit, how bad is it?"

Amelia chuckled. "Bad."

"Some friend you are," Tara hissed.

"Hey, I'm not the one who molested you."

Tara looked at Amelia and then started snickering until they were both laughing hysterically.

"What the hell is up with you two?"

They both straightened to see Fury and Trager standing there.

Tara narrowed her eyes on Traeger and pointed at her neck. "Really?"

She could tell he knew she was talking about the hickeys because he smirked.

He shrugged. "Hey, babe. You tasted so fucking good, I couldn't help it."

Tara watched the light spark in Fury's eyes as he headed Amelia's way. She laughed when her friend held a spatula out.

"Oh, hell no. You keep those lips off my neck."

Fury chuckled. "It will happen. I want my mark on you."

"I think everyone knows you and I are…"

"Yes?" Fury asked with a raised eyebrow.

Tara smiled as she watched a blush overtake Amelia's face.

Fury laughed when Amelia growled. "Later, babe."

Traeger glanced at her. "Skirts, babe. Don't forget."

Amelia glanced at her in confusion.

Tara shook her head and mouthed, "Later."

"Jesus, man, did you try to eat her?" Fury asked Traeger on their way out the back door, which sent them into laughter again.

Chapter Eleven

Tara and Amelia looked around the kitchen one more time.

"Let's go out and sit with the guys," Amelia suggested.

"Sounds good."

Tara followed her to the door but was stopped going through when an arm came around her waist.

"Oh, no, babe. You and I have a date."

A shiver coursed through her at the deep, dark, passion-filled timbre of Traeger's voice.

"A date?" she whispered.

"Yeah, you and me, my bed, now."

She inhaled. "Oh."

He chuckled and lifted her into his arms. She wrapped hers around his neck and stared at him as he carried her up the stairs. He set her down inside his room, turned, and locked the door.

She stepped back and held a hand out. "Wait."

He crossed his arms and scowled. "What?"

"I ... I want to shower."

"You can after."

She shook her head. "I can tell you took one. Please."

He growled. "Fine. I'm giving you five minutes."

Her eyes widened. "Five?"

"You're time's started."

She squeaked and rushed into the bathroom. Quickly, she started the shower, brushed her teeth, put her hair up, undressed, and jumped in. She'd never washed so fast in her life. She had shaved the day before, so fortunately, she didn't have to worry about that.

Tara jumped out, patted herself dry, wrapped the

towel around her midsection, and started putting her lotion on.

The door jerked open, almost making her drop the bottle.

"It has not been five minutes," she complained.

He leaned against the doorjamb and crossed his arms. "No, it hasn't, but I missed you."

She snorted. Her attention caught on the fact he'd taken off his boots, cut, and shirt. She'd seen him earlier that morning, but the bedroom had been dimmed, and she'd just had an orgasm and had been weak.

Now with the bright light of the bathroom, she could see every detail of his sculpted physique with numerous tattoos.

"If you keep looking at me like that, I'm not going to last."

Her gaze flew to his. "How … how am I looking at you?"

"Like I'm the most wonderful thing you've ever seen."

She inhaled. "But you are."

"Fuck." He stepped toward her, picked her up, and walked into the bedroom. Then he tore the towel off her and set her on the mattress.

She exhaled as she watched as he pulled his jeans down.

"Wait."

He growled.

"No," she said and slid to the floor. "I want to help."

"Jesus, woman, you're killing me here."

"You're a tough guy. You can handle it."

He raised his hands out of the way.

He'd pulled most of his zipper down, so she finished it and then started to lower his jeans. She gasped when his cock sprang out and almost hit her in the face.

He stepped out of the jeans, and she tossed them aside.

Before he could stop her, she grabbed his cock and studied it. She would never have thought she'd think a penis was beautiful, but his was. "You're so soft."

He hissed. "I'm not going to last, babe."

"Just let me taste a little."

"Fuck." He looked at the ceiling.

His whole body shook after she swiped the head of his cock with her tongue. She closed her eyes and pulled it into her mouth an inch and then two. She couldn't believe how brave she felt right then.

She'd only gotten to taste him for a moment before he pulled her off him and tossed her on the bed.

"I'll let you suck me off another time, and I guarantee you'll take every drop I give you and beg for more."

A giggle tore from her mouth as she bounced.

"Now I get you."

Before any warning, he spread her legs, dipped his head, and attached his mouth to her cunt.

She screamed and tried to push him off, but he gripped her hips and kept her in place. The first orgasm caught her by surprise and almost scared her. Another scream tore from her as she thrashed on the mattress. He kept at her until she lay limp, and a fine layer of sweat covered her.

He chuckled and crawled up until he covered her. He pressed his mouth against hers, dipping his tongue in to taste every part of her, letting her taste herself. Then he moved lower to take one and then the other tit into his mouth, tormenting them until they stood rigid and red.

Traeger reached for one of the condoms he'd set up at the head of the bed and quickly rolled it on. He nudged her legs apart and made a place for himself in between her thighs.

She tensed and grabbed his waist to hold him off.

"Easy, I'm not going to hurt you."

She shuddered and exhaled. "I … okay."

"I'll go easy on you. All I want you to do is relax and enjoy."

She nodded.

He cupped her face in his hands and spent a few long minutes ramping up her desire again. One hand slid down as he sucked on her tongue to thumb her nipple. He continued to pump his cock against her clit, making her squirm and cry out her need.

She could feel herself coming undone again and began panting.

"That's it."

He pressed the head of his cock into her cunt and slid inch by inch until he bottomed out inside of her. He saw her wince a few times and would stop, but otherwise, she didn't try to fight him.

"There you go. Good girl. I knew you could take me."

She felt dizzy and a bit overwhelmed as she felt him stretch her to the point of pain while his huge body covered her. If he didn't hold himself up off her chest, she wouldn't have been able to breathe.

He bent and kissed her lips, eyebrows, and then went for an ear. "How are you doing?"

She pulled her knees up against his waist and dug her nails into his shoulders.

"I … I think I'm okay."

He chuckled. "You're more than okay, babe. You're fucking fantastic. I'll take it slow this time."

She nodded slowly and braced herself.

He huffed out a breath. "Babe, I'm not going to

hurt you."

She nodded again.

He snorted and then pulled out and pushed in several times at a slow, steady pace. Only when she started to lift her hips did he pick up the pace.

"Oh, please," she whimpered.

"Fuck, I love it when you beg."

She could feel her internal muscles tighten when he sped up. Each thrust was a little harder and faster than the one before. Her heart thumped painfully against her breast, and her breathing turned into panting gasps.

"Come for me, baby. I've got you."

Her body ceased to be her own. She was unable to control her movements or reactions. He played her body like a pro.

A wave of throbbing, intense desire jolted her already overstimulated body, scaring her with its force.

She bucked against him and lost her breath. Lights flashed behind her eyelids as she hung on to him for dear life. When the band that held her at the pinnacle finally snapped, a cry of relief sprang from her mouth. She felt like she was flying, and the only thing holding her steady was Traeger.

She vaguely heard him encourage and reassure her as he took his own pleasure.

When he stopped and held himself over her, she let her arms drop to the side because there was no more strength to be had at the moment. He slid his cock out of her and to the side before he pulled her into his arms. She heard her own labored breathing mixed with his as she drifted to sleep, unable to keep her eyes open anymore.

Chapter Twelve

The next few weeks stayed calm, and Traeger was amazed at how close he and Tara had gotten in such a short amount of time.

That morning, as he left his bed, he took her lips in a kiss so hot and carnal it took his breath away. He was amazed at how hard it was to leave her as she slept naked and with only a thin blanket covering her lower half. He could have sat there all day and just stared at her.

Unreasonable anger at the thought of the power she held over him took him out of the room and downstairs. Traeger thought he'd calmed his anger, but he still felt edgy, and he couldn't figure out why.

That morning, he'd snapped at everyone, so he decided to come out and work on his bike. It always seemed to calm him for some reason. Maybe it was because it kept his mind off everything except what he was doing. He ignored the guys who came into the shop and tried to talk to him. One look from him was all it took.

The day crept by, and he tried to stay out of the kitchen and away from Tara. He wasn't mad at her. She just made him feel … too much.

His stomach rumbled, reminding him he hadn't eaten since the morning. After washing his hands, he walked in the back door. The sound of Tara's laughter was the first thing he heard, and when he saw her taking a pie from the oven, it felt like the air had been sucked out of the room.

This was a dream he'd always had that he convinced himself he'd never achieved—the love of a good woman who made a home for him and baked him pies.

"Traeger, are you okay?"

He focused on Tara as she looked at him worriedly.

When was the last time anyone worried about him?

Jesus, he needed to get away from her. "I'm good. I'll see you later."

"Okay."

He walked away and up to his room, where he showered and then lay down on the bed. He knew he was being a pussy hiding in his room, but until he got his head on straight, he didn't want to face anyone.

Fuck, the happiness on Tara's face was something he hadn't seen on anyone he knew until her. The fact he was part of it made him feel good, but at the same time, it scared the hell out of him.

His stomach started demanding food when he realized it was dinner time. He didn't want to face anyone, but he'd never been a pussy. He'd show them all that she didn't affect him and that he was still his own man.

****

Tara walked outside with Amelia to see the woman Bull brought hanging off Fury. She relaxed when he pushed her down. When she made her way to Traeger, she expected him to do the same thing. Instead, he looked Tara straight in the eyes and put his arm around the woman. Several of the guys looked back and forth between the two.

She felt a burning ball of embarrassment and anger settle in her stomach before she turned her head. Then she turned away and walked over to where Amelia was sitting and put her plate down. She tried to get a few bites down her throat, but they kept getting stuck, so she put down her fork.

"What the hell is Traeger doing?" Amelia asked furiously. "Have you two had a fight?"

Tara looked away from them and down at her plate. Her appetite had flown away. She shook her head. "No. I thought we were fine."

Fury glanced over and cursed, which made her feel better.

"He's a fucking asshole." Fury looked at Tara. "Don't even look over there. You have him running scared."

Tara's gaze jerked up to Fury's. "I haven't done anything."

"Yeah, you have. The same thing this one did to me."

Amelia gasped. "What?"

"Made me fall in love with you."

She looked at Tara. "I believe him. I see the way Traeger looks at you."

Tara pushed the food around on her plate. "He's got a funny way of showing it."

"Just you wait. If you ignore him, he'll come running," Fury said.

"He can do what he wants. We haven't made a commitment."

"You're sleeping together every night," Amelia said.

"Not anymore." She stood, making sure she didn't look his way. "I'm going to go start on the dishes."

"I'll be right in."

She nodded and headed toward the back door. She could feel Traeger's gaze follow her, but she ignored him.

When she heard the back door open and close, she had her hands in sudsy water. "I've got the pots done if you want to start handing me the plates."

When no one said anything, she turned and found Traeger standing at the island with his hands on top and his eyes boring into hers.

They stared at each other for a moment.

"You better get back out to your whore. This one is a little busy."

Dark anger crossed his face before he turned and walked back out.

Tara sighed, and her shoulders slumped. She couldn't make the pain lessen, but then the betrayal was very new.

She had to come to grips with the fact they'd never be together. The problem she had was she didn't want to be alone, but there was no other man in the club she could see herself with. To see Traeger with woman after woman would make her physically ill.

She tensed when the door opened again but relaxed when she realized it was Amelia.

"How are you doing?" Amelia asked her and wrapped an arm around her waist.

"I'll handle it. Eventually."

"He's a fucking bastard, and you deserve better than him."

"I'm starting to think that, too."

Tara continued to wash the dishes but paused when Amelia stiffened and growled.

She glanced over her shoulder to see Traeger with his arm around the whore again, walking through the kitchen with his eyes on her. She turned back to the sink and concentrated on the dish.

That hurt enough, but then the woman talked about him not wanting a fatty. Tara knew she was just being a bitch, but the fact Traeger didn't say anything told her a lot.

"What a prick," Amelia hissed.

Tara couldn't agree with her more, but she was afraid to voice anything because she'd burst into tears. She laid the towel over the sink to dry and looked around for anything else that needed to be done.

Fury came in the door. He walked to Amelia and wrapped an arm around her waist. She was so happy for her friend and hoped one day she would find a man who loved her as much as Fury loved Amelia.

"Hey, Fury. Is there a room I can use?"

Fury sighed. "He's only being a douche because he's scared. I'll talk to him."

"I really wish you wouldn't." Tara wrapped her arms around her waist. "It's been several weeks, and he hasn't made a commitment, so I need to move on."

"You'll leave the club?" Fury asked.

Tara looked at Amelia. "I hate that I'd leave you to do all the work."

"Don't worry about me, hun. You can't stay here if you're not happy. I can help you look for a job and a place to live tomorrow."

Tara nodded. "That would be great." She turned back to Fury. "Is there a room I can use for now?"

Fury sighed and shook his head. "Let me go check. I'll be right back."

Amelia looked at her after Fury left. "You know everything I said was bullshit, right?"

"Yes," Tara said and tried to smile. "You think Fury will tell Traeger, and he'll try to keep me here, but it's not going to happen."

"God, the thought of you not being here scares the hell out of me."

"I don't want to leave either, but I don't have a choice. I have a feeling no other man here would touch me because they'll always see me as Traeger's. And the thought of having to see him with other women would kill me."

Fury came back in. "The second-from-the-last door on the left. It has a bed and dresser you can use. Grab some pillows and blankets out of the hall closet."

"Thank you."

Tara hugged Amelia and walked upstairs, not looking anywhere but in front of her. She went up to the room she'd been using with Traeger and grabbed some of her things. She planned on going back the next day to get the rest.

After a shower, she dropped into bed.

She didn't think she could sleep, but the stress of the day pulled her down. She woke up an hour or so later to find the pillow wet from tears she'd shed when she was asleep. After flipping the pillow to the dry side, she laid her head back down and closed her eyes.

Chapter Thirteen

Traeger watched Tara take the stairs and felt like the biggest douche alive. She'd done nothing to deserve his treatment. The fact most of his brothers looked at him with disgust didn't help.

The woman currently sitting on his lap smelled like shit, and he couldn't take the sound of her voice any longer. He stood abruptly, dumping her on the floor.

"You fucking bastard," she screamed.

He looked down at her in disgust. "Shut up, you filthy whore. Get out of my sight and don't fucking touch me again."

"What is your fucking problem?" she yelled. "You're the one who came on to me."

"Wrong. You couldn't pay me enough to fuck your skanky ass."

One of the other men grabbed her when she went for him.

He didn't care. He just turned and walked off as he heard one of his brothers try to calm her. "Woman, you don't want to be fucking with him, especially when he's in this mood."

Before he made it to the stairs, Fury called out to him. "Office, now."

Fuck, this was all he needed. He knew he'd fucked up, and he didn't want his prez flying into him.

Fury closed the door after he went in.

"Have a seat."

He grunted, sat, leaned back, and crossed his arms over his chest. "What's up?"

"I don't know what the fuck is going on with you, but when it affects my woman, it pisses me off."

"Wait, how the hell is this affecting Amelia?"

"It seems she's going to help Tara find a job and a place to live tomorrow, and I've never seen her this upset for her friend."

Traeger jerked to stand in front of Fury's desk as his heart pounded out of control, his body was tense. "What? No, she's not going anywhere."

"Yeah, she is, and you're not going to stop her."

"Like fuck I'm not. She stays here with me."

Fury sat back and studied him. "Do you want to tell me why you were with that fucking whore and rubbing it in Tara's face?"

Traeger ran a hand down his face as he cursed. He knew whatever he said would never go to anyone else. Not even Amelia.

"I fucking freaked out this morning. I was staring at Tara, and I realized how much fucking power she holds over me. I've never let anyone have control of me, but just by her smiling at me, I'd bend over backward to make her happy."

Fury nodded. "I get it. I feel the same way about my woman."

"How'd you get past it?"

"I asked myself if I'd rather be alone without Amelia and not have any of the happiness I've found with her because I get a bit freaked out from time to time—or have her in my life, loving and taking care of me and dealing with my fear. It's a no-brainer. I know I probably don't deserve her, but goddammit, she's mine, and I'm not giving her up."

Traeger felt a weight was lifted off his shoulders at that moment. It helped to know his closest friend was going through the same thing and that he'd have him to talk to when he got overwhelmed again.

There was no way he could live without Tara. She was his world, and he needed to tell her that. He nodded.

"Thanks, man."

"Is your head out of your ass now?"

Traeger chuckled. "Yeah, as much as it can be."

"Good. You've got a bunch of sucking up to do. I've been there, and it can be done. Right now, I've got an old lady that I want to cheer up and then fuck blind."

Traeger laughed. "I'm on my way. I'll see you in the morning."

"Night."

Traeger took the stairs two at a time and walked into his room to find Tara not there and the bed still made. Fear hit him hard. God, he couldn't have lost her already. There was no fucking way he'd let her go.

He sprinted downstairs where several of the guys were still partying.

"Has anyone seen Tara?"

"I thought I saw her go into the second-from-the-last bedroom. I thought it was strange, but I didn't say anything. But then someone told me you were all over the whore tonight, so I figured you guys broke up."

"Fuck that. I wasn't all over the whore. Whose room is that?" His voice had turned deadly. Fuck, the thought of one of his brothers getting his hands on her made him beyond furious, more like homicidal.

"It's empty, man," Bear told him.

He relaxed. "Thanks." He walked away. Within a minute, he stood in front of the door and tried to open it, finding it locked.

"Goddammit."

He pulled his knife out of his pocket and used it to jimmy the door. He could just make out her body under the blanket. He closed and locked the door again before he undressed and slipped into bed, curling around her.

He kissed her cheek and the side of her neck as his hand caressed her breast, waiting for her to wake up.

Tara slowly woke up, and he could see and feel the moment she remembered his betrayal. She tried to get away from him, and he restrained her underneath him, holding her hands over her head and pinning her to the mattress.

"You fucking bastard. Get the fuck off me. You're never touching me again after being with that woman."

"I wasn't with her."

"I knew you lied about wanting me and liking my figure, but why'd you have to play with me?" She sobbed and tried to hit him. "God, I hate you."

"Listen to me. I didn't fuck the whore."

"I don't care what you did. You showed me without words and in the meanest way possible how much I mean to you. Now get the fuck off."

"I'm sorry."

"I don't fucking care," she cried. After struggling for another moment, she relaxed and turned her head away from him, and let the tears come. "Just go," she murmured.

"I'm not leaving you. I fucked up."

When he caught the pain in her eyes, he felt like a total prick. "I'm sorry. I don't want anyone else. I just want you."

She tried to laugh. "You've got a funny way of showing it." She started to struggle again.

"Settle down before you hurt yourself," he said with a growl.

"You don't get to tell me what to do anymore, Traeger. Go back to the whore."

"I don't want the fucking whore," he shouted. "I love you. I want you."

She snorted.

He knew she didn't believe him, and that was his

own fault.

"No, listen to me. Did you see me, the way I looked when I came into the kitchen this afternoon as you were laughing about something and pulling a pie from the oven?"

She still wouldn't look at him. "Yes. I asked if you were okay."

"Yes. I wasn't, though. I had just realized that I loved you more than anyone I ever had before in my life."

"Except your girlfriend that died, Paula."

He remembered he had told her about the woman late one night as they sat outside with her on his lap. "No, babe, even Paula. That's what freaked me out. I lost it after she died, but I started thinking that I'd die with you if I lost you. I wouldn't be able to go on. I love the club, and they have to come first sometimes, but the rest of the time, I'm yours."

He could tell she still didn't believe him. "Tell me this. What would happen if you lost me?"

"I already did," she murmured with a sob.

"Goddammit, you didn't fucking lose me," he yelled. "I was being an asshole, and I'm sorry. I won't ever do it again. Now answer the fucking question."

"I don't know. It terrifies me to think of you not being a part of my world."

"I feel the same about you, if not worse, baby. Please forgive me. I swear I won't ever do something like that again."

"I don't know…"

He cupped her face in his hands to keep her facing him. "Don't you dare give up on me," he said fiercely. "As far as your body goes, I love everything about it. Don't ever think I don't. You should be able to tell from the way I can't keep my hands off you."

She started crying.

"Shhh, hush, baby. God, I hate that I hurt you. I won't let you go."

She sniffed. "I love you."

"I love you, too. Will you forgive me?"

Her answer took a while, and the whole time, he sweated, hoping he hadn't fucked it up forever.

She nodded slowly. "But I won't be able to handle that again. If you touch another woman, I'm done. I saw what men having affairs did to the women I grew up knowing, and I won't let that happen to me. No matter how much I love you."

"I won't." He pressed his forehead against hers.

"How does Bull feel about that whore hanging all over you all?"

"He doesn't give a shit. She approached him at a bar, and he thought she was hot. She wanted to become one of the whores, so he brought her back here. When she found out who the president and vice president were, she came after us first."

"Is that normal?"

"Maybe. Women like men of power." He bent down and kissed her. "Can we not talk about her anymore? I need to be inside of you."

She pulled him on top of her and wrapped her arms around his shoulders. "Yes."

"You're my old lady, babe."

"What?"

"I'll let everyone know tomorrow. You're never getting away from me."

"I never tried to," she said and started to cry again.

He gathered her in his arms, pushed her legs apart, and slammed into her, making them both cry out.

"Shhh, I've got you," he murmured against her

ear. "I love you, babe."

She sniffed. "I love you, too."

He began pumping inside of her, gaining speed and force with every thrust until she was writhing under him and begging to come.

"Yes, baby. Come for me."

She screamed and dug her nails into his shoulders, making him hiss with the pain that brought him only more pleasure.

"That's it. A bit more."

He finally let himself go, slamming into her over and over as he came. Once he was drained, he held himself over her as he tried to get his heart and breathing under control enough to move. Finally, after a long moment, he pulled out. He wrapped her in the blanket and walked them back to his bedroom.

"Why are we moving?" she asked.

"I want you in my bed," he said simply.

She was out by the time he got them into bed, with the door locked and the lights off.

He finally sighed in relief. She was where she was supposed to be, and his head was back on straight. He couldn't ask for more than that.

Chapter Fourteen

For the next few months, things stayed peaceful, especially after Rissa, the woman Bull had brought, left.

But then Ax brought home a woman. This one was as bad if not worse than Rissa.

Carlee was a total bitch to everyone, but especially Amelia and her, and her insults were getting old. Tara thought about going to Traeger, but they decided to put up with her behavior because Ax seemed so happy. They didn't want him to lose her if that was what he wanted.

"Is lunch about ready?"

Tara glanced at Amelia and rolled her eyes. Carlee was about as skanky as any woman they'd ever seen, and her attitude made her even uglier.

The woman kept pushing them, and if one of the guys overheard, Fury and Traeger would know within minutes.

"Lunch for the guys will be ready in a few minutes, but you're going to have to figure out your own," Amelia said.

Tara was shocked by the hatred in the woman's expression.

"When Ax is the president, you fucking cunts will be out of here."

Tara gasped in shock. Jesus, talking like that could get her killed.

"If I were you, I wouldn't be going around saying shit like that," Tara advised her.

"Fuck you."

"Where did you get the idea Ax would ever be President?" Amelia asked.

"Me. I think he'd make a better president than

Fury."

Tara listened to Amelia ask if she'd talked to Ax about it, and she really wanted to know the answer to that too.

"No, not yet," Carlee said with a smirk.

"If I were you, the sooner you talk to him, the better," Amelia told her.

Carlee hissed at them and talked about how much better she was than they were, and Tara had to hold her tongue.

She looked at Amelia to see the worry in her eyes.

"I say one word to Fury, and you'll disappear, and I'm not talking about getting thrown out of the club. If you are as smart as you say you are, you wouldn't be disrespecting the old ladies of the club."

"Fuck that," Carlee hissed. "If I'm an old lady fighting with another, they'll leave us alone."

Tara smirked. "But … bitch, you're not and never will be an old lady of this club."

"Fuck you."

Tara tensed when Traeger and Fury walked in. Traeger looked back and forth, and she scrambled to find what to say when he asked.

"Is there a problem, baby?"

"No, we're good." Tara shook her head.

Her heartbeat accelerated when he stalked her.

"If you're lying to me, and I find out, your ass will be so hot you won't be able to sit for a week."

"I'm not lying, Traeger. You know how women are."

He snorted. "Yeah, you're all bitches."

Oh, my God. She couldn't believe he just said that. "Hey!"

"Not you, though, baby," he murmured against her lips.

She snorted but let him deepen the kiss.

Carlee walked out of the kitchen, and Tara didn't see her for several hours. She was always on her guard when Carlee showed up because she knew it wouldn't be an enjoyable interaction. She was hoping that every time the bitch left, it would be the last time she ever saw her.

For the next few days, Tara kept her eyes on Ax and Carlee when they were together. She caught no deception from Ax at all.

When Tara and Amelia both got patted on the shoulder as the men made their way outside after grabbing sandwiches from them, she smiled.

"Thanks, mamas," they all said.

Traeger came up behind her and wrapped his arms around her.

"How are you doing, babe?"

"Good. Is it okay if I go see my mom tomorrow?"

Traeger nodded. "Yeah, I'm not busy, so I'll go with you."

"Do you think this time you'll want to meet her?"

Traeger shrugged. "We'll see."

Tara pulled his head down and kissed him. "I'll understand if you don't."

She'd gone to see her mother numerous times, but mostly, the other guys went with her and stood outside, or if Traeger did, he stood by the car to wait. She understood. It was probably hard for him to see her mother and how much they loved each other, although her mother's emotions hadn't been apparent for a long time.

"Call if you need me," he said and walked out the back.

"Get a room," someone said when they saw Fury all over Amelia, making Tara laugh.

Tara's head snapped up when Fury growled.

"Why the fuck aren't you helping them?" he asked Carlee.

Carlee raised her nose in the air. "They've got it handled."

Tara bit her lip to keep from laughing when Fury shook his head and grumbled, "Fucking worthless," before he walked out.

Tara gasped when Burn walked into the kitchen and barked at Carlee after catching her expression before she could mask it. She hadn't really been paying attention to the bitch because she was too busy making sandwiches for the guys, and they all ate several at a time.

"You're not fucking looking at these two like that, are you?"

Tara's stomach dropped at the anger on Burn's face.

"Answer me," he said when she didn't speak.

"No, of course not," Carlee said nervously.

If Tara didn't know how protective he was over them, she'd be terrified of him. The man had a look like he could cut your throat and then step over you when you fell at his feet. She didn't know what his story was, but what she had surmised from the few things the other guys said, he'd had a really rough childhood. Worse than Traeger's.

He glanced her way. "Is she bothering you girls?"

They shook their heads.

"No, everything's good," Amelia said quickly.

Burn pointed a finger at Carlee. "I'm watching your ass, bitch. I haven't liked you from the start. Why Ax wants your raunchy ass is beyond me. You're nothing but a fucking skank."

Carlee gasped, turned abruptly, and walked out.

Tara continued to make the food and pretend everything was good.

"If that bitch gives you any problem, tell me."

God, the sound of his voice was enough to scare the hell out of her.

"Sure, Burn," Tara said. "How many sandwiches do you want?"

"Two for now."

Tara handed him a plate.

"If I find out she's messing with you and you don't tell any of us, I'll make sure your men punish you enough that you won't ever lie to me again."

Tara exhaled when he left.

"What are we going to do?" Tara asked as she pressed on her stomach.

"I don't know. If we say anything, she'll disappear, and I don't want to be responsible for her death."

"Me either, but I think she could pose a threat."

"Let's tell them if anything else happens, okay?"

Tara nodded. "I like that idea."

"Women, get your asses out here," a voice yelled from the backyard.

The time that she had been with the club had opened her eyes to so many things. She'd always been told motorcycle clubs were terrible and that all the men were druggies and raped women. Yes, they were all scary in their own ways. They went by a certain code. It wasn't like she was taught, but she couldn't see any of them raping a woman or intentionally hurting someone for the thrill of it.

Tara laughed at something one of the guys said as she ate her sandwich. It seemed more and more each day, her world was becoming lighter and happier. Oh, she still worried her mom, but she knew she was in good hands and was happy. That was all that mattered.

Chapter Fifteen

"Babe, let's go," Traeger yelled up the stairs.

Tara rushed down the hallway and then the stairs. "I'm coming. I had to get my list."

He wrapped an arm around her waist. "What list?"

"Grocery." She giggled when she caught his grumpy look. "I know you hate the store. I can always go with someone else."

He put the SUV in drive and pulled out. "No, as long as you don't spend hours in there. How much time are we staying for your mom?"

"They won't let me stay more than thirty minutes, but that's on a good day, and she doesn't have many of those anymore."

Tara looked out her side window and blinked several times to dispel the tears that were quickly filling them.

She felt Traeger's hand grasp hers after she sniffed.

"I wish I could make this better for you. You know I would if I could."

She looked his way. "I know, but you just being here is enough."

He lifted her hand and kissed her knuckles. They rode the rest of the way in silence.

Traeger came around and lifted her out of the vehicle and then took her hand. Tara inhaled deeply to try to settle her heart as she followed him into the building. She was pleased he'd decided to come in with her.

They walked up to the desk.

"Hello, my name is Tara Downey. I'm here to see Donna Downey."

"Just one moment. If you'd like to wait in the reception area, there is free coffee."

"Thank you."

Traeger pulled her over and wrapped an arm around her shoulders.

Tara leaned against him and noticed the looks they got. She should be used to it, but some of the people looked at Traeger in disgust, and they didn't even know him.

"Tara," said a woman headed her way.

"Hi, Nicole."

She moved them away from the other people in the waiting area.

"Hello, you must be Traeger." Nicole smiled.

He nodded.

She turned back to Tara. "I'm sorry. I thought someone called you. She's not doing well right now."

Tara's eyes filled with tears. "But I called just a little bit ago."

Nicole reached out for her hand. "I know, hun. We just had to sedate her. Her blood pressure was extremely high, and we worried about a stroke."

"What did that?"

Nicole shrugged. "It could be so many things. I couldn't guess. If you'd like to wait a few minutes until the sedative is in effect, you can come back and see her. She won't be able to be awake, but she seems to get more agitated when she's awake."

Tara looked at Traeger. "Can we wait?"

Nicole looked back and forth. "I suggest you do, hun. She's not going to be with us very much longer."

Tara nodded. "Yeah, I've come to grips with that."

Traeger stroked the back of her head. "Of course, we can, babe."

"I'll come back and get you." Nicole turned and walked off.

Traeger wrapped his arms around her and stood silently.

Within five minutes, Nicole was back. "Come this way, you guys."

Tara and Traeger followed the nurse down a few hallways until they got to her mom's room.

Tara sucked in a deep, steadying breath "Why does she change with every visit?"

Nicole smoothed the woman's blanket. "She's thinner now. She's stopped eating, so we have to give her nutrients in an IV."

Tara nodded. "I was told that was happening." She walked over to the side of the bed and reached for her mother's hand. She vaguely heard Nicole tell Traeger she'd be back to check on them.

"Oh, Mama. I'm going to miss you. Hell, I already do. I can't remember the last time you looked at me and said my name."

Tara wiped a tear that slid down her cheek. The breath shuddered out of her when she felt Traeger's presence against her back as he wrapped an arm around her waist.

They stood like that for several minutes while Tara touched her mom and talked about what she was up to and how much she wanted her to meet Traeger.

She wiped the tears away. "Mama, I'm going to go. I'll try to be back before you go to Daddy." She bent forward and slipped an arm around her frail mom. "If you go sooner, go in peace and know you were the best mom a person could ever have. You don't have to fight anymore. Go to Daddy, and I'll see you soon," Tara whispered in her mom's ear and gently kissed her dry paper-thin cheek. "I love you, Mama."

She stood, took one more long look at her mom, turned, and walked out with Traeger close beside her. On the way out, Tara thanked everyone she saw and gave Nicole and a few other hugs.

A few feet out the door, Tara stopped and looked up at the clear blue sky. She took several breaths and then let Traeger lead her to the vehicle, where he leaned against it and pulled her into his arms.

"Cry, baby. Let it all out. I'm right here."

Tara grabbed his shirt and let out a distressed cry before the sobs tore from her throat. She didn't know how long they stood there as she cried, but the storm of emotion passed, leaving her limp.

Traeger held her tightly with one arm and his other hand. He petted her and rubbed her back at the same time he murmured his love to her and that he'd take care of her.

She took a step back and dug through her purse for a tissue. Then she wiped her face and blew her nose before she stuck it back in her purse. She looked up and tried to smile. "I must look awful right now."

He tipped her chin up and pressed a kiss to her mouth. "You'll always be beautiful to me, babe."

"God, I love you."

He grinned. "I know."

She sputtered out and hit him on the chest.

"Good. I was missing that smile," he murmured.

She squeezed him. "Thank you for being here."

"I'll always be here for you."

She grinned up at him. "I know."

He laughed and started moving her to the passenger door. After lifting her in, he leaned in and kissed her again.

"Do you still want to go to the store?"

She nodded. "Yeah. It will get my mind off

things."

"All right." He started the SUV and pulled out in traffic.

Chapter Sixteen

"What are they doing here?" Tara asked as they pulled into the grocery store parking lot. Bear and Rage sat leaning against their bikes with their arms crossed.

Tara watched from the vehicle as the people put distance between the bikers and them. She would have felt sorry for the guys, but the assholes actually liked scaring most people.

"I told them to meet us."

"Why?"

"Babe, I take your safety very seriously."

She almost rolled her eyes but knew it would just piss him off. Traeger helped her out and then took her hand.

She waved and smiled as she passed them. "Hey, Rage and Bear."

"Hey, mama," they both said, making her smile.

Traeger got a cart and then walked alongside her as she shopped. Traeger had put Rage in front and Bear behind them.

It was clear to everyone that they were protecting her, and she saw people's curious looks as though they wondered who she was.

At the end, Traeger cussed as he paid the bill, making Tara snicker.

"If Bear hadn't kept adding things to the cart, we would have walked out of here with half the total," she told him.

Traeger snorted as he put his card away in his wallet. "Note to self, don't bring Bear to the store."

Rage and Tara chuckled, and Bear frowned.

In the parking lot, Traeger got her into the vehicle while the other two loaded up the groceries.

Tara gasped when she saw a man slap a woman

across the face and knock her down onto the hard concrete.

"Oh, my God, Traeger. Can we help her?"

"Stay here," he ordered. Traeger was out of the vehicle and in front of the man within seconds. Tara bit her lip because she wanted to go to the weeping woman who held her face and cowered against the car, but knew she'd be in deep shit because Traeger told her to stay in the vehicle.

She couldn't hear anything. They were talking too softly. Bear stood by the SUV, protecting her, and Rage walked over.

Then she watched Rage try to talk to the woman. He got in between her and the man Traeger was talking to.

The woman nodded at something Rage said. Tara was surprised when she took the hand Rage held out to her. Rage was a handsome guy if you could see past the scowl and tattoos.

He brought her toward the SUV and then opened the back door. "Hey, mama, I'm sending a chickadee with you to the compound. I want you and Amelia to take care of her and show her the way."

"She's moving in with us?" Tara asked in surprise.

"Yup. She has to. It's destined. Guess what her name is?"

She smiled at the look of smug satisfaction on his face.

"What?" Tara asked.

"It's Harley."

Tara laughed. "I agree. She definitely needs to be in our family." She looked at the timid but beautiful woman. "Are you okay about going home with us?"

She nodded. "Yes. Ted, my ex, keeps finding me.

He won't ever leave me alone, and I know he's going to kill me someday."

Tara reached out and took the woman's hand. "That won't happen if you're with us. These guys will take care of you."

"I'm not imposing?" Harley asked.

Rage answered. "No, we've got plenty of room. Don't we, Tara?"

Tara smiled. She'd never seen Rage like this, and she thought it was great. "He's absolutely right, Harley."

"When we get back home, few guys and I will come and get your stuff."

"It's all in that car." She pointed to a small red, late-model SUV. "I just pulled into town. I was hoping to stay a few weeks, but he caught up with me quickly."

"We'll come and get it when we get you safe."

Tara glanced back to see Traeger squatting by the man lying on the ground with his head on the curb with blood coming out of his nose and lip. Good, the bastard deserved everything he got.

Traeger lifted the man off the ground with one hand and shook him. Whatever he said scared the guy because he ran as soon as Traeger let him loose.

Then Traeger got back into the vehicle and turned to look at the woman. "How are you doing?"

"I'm okay. It's been so much worse. I can't thank you enough for saving me."

"That shit doesn't happen in our town if we can help it."

The woman cupped her injured cheek.

Tara smiled. "When we get back home, I'll get you an ice pack." She saw a sheen of tears in the woman's eyes.

"Thank you."

They pulled up into the compound and parked.

Traeger got out and whistled, which brought several guys to the vehicle.

Tara caught the shock and then fear in Harley's eyes. She reached back and took her hand.

"Hey, Harley, you're okay here. No one will hurt you, and if anyone gives you grief, tell me, but I can't see that happening. It's a really great group of guys. They look rough, but they've always been gentle with me."

Harley nodded and then jumped when her door opened.

Tara noticed her relax when she saw it was Rage. She turned when her door opened, and Traeger lifted her out. She patted his chest. "Did you get hurt at all?"

He snorted. "I should beat your ass for that insult."

She grinned. "I'm sorry. You know I worry about you."

He kissed her forehead. "Yeah, I do. Now go hide the groceries before Bear finds them."

"I heard that," Bear yelled, making Tara giggle.

Amelia was already in the kitchen, taking things out of the bags when Rage pulled Harley in, and Tara followed behind.

Tara walked over to Amelia. "Hey, we have a new addition to the family."

Amelia looked around and smiled.

"Her name is Harley, and Rage wants us to take care of her."

Amelia walked to Harley and held out a hand while Tara got a cold pack from the freezer.

"Harley, why don't you sit down and put this on while Amelia and I deal with the groceries."

"Thank you."

Amelia looked back and forth. "So, what happened?"

"My ex-boyfriend was slapping me around when these guys showed up and saved me."

"I'm so glad they were there," Amelia said.

"I am, too. Traeger took care of him," Tara told her.

"Good."

Tara and Amelia continued to put the groceries away and talk to Harley, trying to calm her fears as the men walked in and out.

Tara saw her smile when Bear came in and grabbed the package of Oreos stuck them under his arm. "These are mine," he said.

Tara snickered. "You better hide them before anyone else sees them."

"Damn right," he said.

The three women watched him try to hide them as he walked out of the kitchen. They looked at each other and then laughed.

"See," Tara told Harley. "Just like regular guys." That sent them to chuckling again.

Tara saw the woman relax even more and knew she'd be okay with a little help from her and Amelia and, of course, Rage.

Chapter Seventeen

Tara was wiping the last pot when her phone rang. "Hello?"

"Tara, It's Nicole, hun. Your mom passed away about five minutes ago. I'm so sorry."

Tara stared out the window and swallowed. "Thank you, Nicole. I'll make the arrangements for her."

"She was a sweet woman, and I can tell how much you loved each other. She'll be here when you are ready. Just have the funeral home come to get her."

Tara cleared her throat. "I will. Thank you again for taking such good care of her."

"You're welcome. Call if there's anything you need."

"I will."

Amelia found her staring out the window with her phone in her hands. "Hey, what's going on?"

Tara looked at her friend. "Mom's gone."

Amelia gasped, and her eyes filled with tears before she pulled Tara into her arms and held her for a long time.

People came and went, but both girls ignored them.

"What can I do?"

"Can I talk to Fury? Traeger left this morning, and I need to talk to him. He only carried the phone Fury gives him."

"Let's go. I think he's in the office."

Amelia knocked and waited for Fury's approval.

"Come in," Fury said and leaned back in his chair. "Hey, what's going on, girls?"

Tara took a breath. "My mom died."

"Oh, hell, I'm sorry." He stood and came around

the desk, pulled both in his arms, and held them for a long moment before sitting back on his desktop. "What can I do?"

"Can I talk to Traeger?"

Tara saw the hard look that crossed Fury's face. Amelia must have seen it also because she stiffened.

Fury wiped a hand down his face. "The thing is, he's in the middle of something, and I don't want him distracted."

Tara thought about that for a moment. "Could he be hurt?"

"There's a possibility, although my guys are always very careful. You might make him take his mind off of what he's supposed to do."

She shook her head. "No. I don't want to distract him. I'll wait until he gets home. I don't know when that is, though."

"Fuck, hun. It could be three days or three weeks."

"He never told me he'd be gone that long."

"He didn't know until he got there."

"What should I do if he calls me?"

Fury's jaw bunched. "He won't. He'll call me if he needs something, but other than that, they're forbidden to talk or call anyone until they're done."

"So, I might not even talk to him for three weeks?"

Fury nodded. "Yeah, I'm sorry."

Amelia squeezed her shoulder. "I can be there with you."

"You'll both have tight security. I can go with you to set everything up, and then during the funeral, I'll also have several guys there. We'll spare no expense for this. You won't be alone. I can promise you that."

Tara nodded. "I appreciate that, and I'll take your

help."

"Good. Why don't you and Amelia plan it, and I can make the calls? When do you want it? Do you want to wait until he gets home?"

She shook her head. "No, we don't know what day that will be, and I don't want to wait. That would be okay, right?"

"Sure."

Amelia grabbed her hand. "I know of the places you need. The ones I used for Dad. They were wonderful."

"Yes. That sounds good." She turned back to Fury. "Thank you."

"You're welcome."

Within three days, everything was set up, and Tara was standing by her mother's gravesite with ten club members, a few nurses, and a few of her mother's friends. Amelia stood on one side of her and Harley on the other. They held her hands the whole time as the preacher droned on about her mother's spirit and God, and Tara knew she wouldn't remember any of it.

At the end, everyone hugged and paid their condolences before heading home.

She didn't know how long she stared at the coffin before a car backfiring made her jump. Tara and Amelia gasped when guys surrounded them, and they started to move them toward the vehicles at a fast pace.

"What's going on?"

"Didn't you hear it?" Bear asked as he looked around the area.

"What? The car?"

"No, that wasn't a car. It was a gun," Fury told them with a black rage in his tone that sent a shiver up Tara's back.

She shivered at the murderous looks as the men

scanned the area.

They got them back to the compound and inside before they relaxed. By then, Tara had a massive headache and just wanted to lie down. "I'm going to go upstairs and lie down for a bit."

Amelia hugged her. "I'll bring some aspirin and juice up. Part of your headache might be because you haven't eaten today."

Tara hugged her back. "Thank you."

"Go and lie down."

Tara dragged herself upstairs, stripped, put her hair up, and jumped into the shower. The heat helped her headache, and the water soothed her. When it started getting cool, she got out, dried off, and pulled on her robe.

She saw Amelia closing the blinds and drapes, darkening the room.

"Thank you."

Amelia smiled at her over her shoulder. "The aspirin and juice are on the nightstand."

Tara downed both, pulled back the covers, and slid in.

Amelia walked over and pulled the blanket up to her chin. "Do you want me to stay here with you?"

"No. But thank you. I just want to sleep for a bit."

Amelia smoothed the hair from her face. "Call for me if you need me, but I'll be checking in on you periodically."

"Okay."

Tara rolled over and was asleep before Amelia closed the bedroom door.

Chapter Eighteen

"Where the fuck is she?" someone bellowed from the front door.

Tara and Amelia glanced at each other and then rushed out to see what the problem was.

Tara gasped with her hand over her mouth when she caught sight of Traeger standing in the middle of the living area beside Fury. She guessed he'd told Traeger about her mom from the look on his face.

Her eyes ate him up. It seemed like months since they'd been together instead of the thirteen days. He looked tired, and his hair was a bit longer.

Her eyes stung when he looked at her and opened his arms.

A whimper burst from her mouth as she ran to him and jumped into his arms. They closed tightly around her, and he pressed his face against her neck.

She hadn't known how much she needed him until she was in his arms.

****

"Fuck, babe, I'm so fucking sorry about your mom and not being here for you."

"I don't care. I'm just glad you're home now."

"Fury, I'll talk to you later. Right now, I need to have my woman under me."

Fury chuckled. "I understand. I'm the same way. Go."

Traeger ran up the stairs with her in his arms. He kicked their door closed and set her on the bed. He stripped her quickly and then himself and had her under him within two minutes. He took her mouth like he was starved for her.

He trapped her head between his two hands.

"We'll talk, babe, but after I fuck you blind."

"God, yes." She arched and begged him to take her.

He positioned his cock and slammed into her. Then he stayed still for a moment to let her get accustomed to him before he started fucking her. The feeling of her wet tight cunt around his cock made him growl with satisfaction. There was no place on earth he'd rather be than inside of her.

He rode her through one and then two orgasms. Dragging screams and begging from her.

"God, woman. I feel your cream sliding down my balls." He kissed her several times and then flipped her onto her stomach, pulled her hips up, and rammed back into her cunt from behind.

He used his fingers to lift her juice up to coat her ass at the same time he fucked her cunt hard. When he was sure she was lubed enough, he pulled out of her pussy to press the tip to her puckered opening.

"Take it easy. You know how to do this. Just relax."

He saw her grip the blanket under her, but she did loosen her ass enough for him to slide in.

"Jesus, woman, you feel so fucking good. I missed you so fucking much."

"I missed you, too," she cried out.

He kept working his cock into her tight ass until he was as far into her as he could get.

"There, babe. You took all of me."

She nodded. "Please, Traeger."

He grasped her hips tightly enough he knew she'd carry bruises the next day, and he always loved to have his mark on her as much as he could. He loved that she never complained about them.

The tight clasp of her internal muscles strangled

his cock so much he knew he wouldn't last long. He started slow and easy, but his thrusts quickly turned hard and fast.

"Fuck, baby, I need you to come for me." He reached under her and started flicking her clit as he continued to pound into her.

When she started to come, he had to force his cock into her because she tightened so much.

The sounds of her screams and moans were music to his ears, something he craved daily.

A tingling sensation started at the base of his spine and moved up. A groan tore from his mouth when he came, filling her up and making her whimper. He continued to thrust until his cock softened inside of her, and he wasn't able to catch his breath. Then he braced himself on one hand and slowly regained enough control to pull out of her.

He winced when she flinched in pain. "I'm sorry, baby," he murmured against her shoulder and then kissed the back of her head. "Relax, and I'll be right back."

When she fell to the side and hummed, he grinned. He was always satisfied when he fucked his woman unconscious.

He flew through a shower and then grabbed a wet washcloth and cleaned the sweat and their combined cum off of her. After he threw the cloth in the bathroom sink, he slid in beside her, wrapping his body around her.

"I'm so glad I'm home, babe," he said against her head. She hummed but otherwise didn't speak. That was okay. He knew she missed him, too. He didn't like the fact he'd left her for so long, but one of the presidents had to be there for the shipment of drugs. It was a huge moneymaker for them, and they couldn't take a chance of it getting it messed up.

He just hoped it would be a long time before he

had to be gone for so long again. Not only was he getting too old for it, but he also thought the younger brothers should take up the slack more when the job wasn't as important as the one he just did.

He and Fury had also been talking about opening up a few businesses in town, like a gym and a pawnshop. With them and the other businesses they owned in town, like the car garage and laundromat, they would be able to cut out the drug runs altogether.

Then he'd never have to be away from her.

The more they thought about the idea, the more they liked it.

Chapter Nineteen

Traeger had been home a week when, one morning, he kissed the back of her shoulder, waking her up.

She turned to see him sitting on the edge of the mattress, dressed. Then she looked at the window and saw it was still dark.

"What are you doing?"

"I have some things to do, but I didn't want to leave without a kiss."

She smiled and wrapped her arms around his neck.

His mouth settled on hers, and it quickly grew hungry. "Jesus, woman, I just fucked you four times last night, and my cock still gets hard."

"I hope that's a good thing, right?"

"Yeah, I just hope it doesn't kill me."

Tara giggled.

He gave her one more kiss. "Go back to sleep."

"Be careful."

He turned at the door. "I always am, babe."

Tara tried for an hour to fall back asleep and finally gave up, dressed, and went downstairs to the kitchen. It wasn't long before Amelia came through the door.

"Wow, you're up early."

Tara smiled over her shoulder as she flipped pancakes. "Yeah, Traeger had to leave early, and I couldn't fall back to sleep."

Amelia poured herself a cup of coffee and then pulled bacon from the refrigerator. "I know how that is. I don't sleep well at all when Fury is away."

They chatted as they made breakfast, keeping it in

the warm oven for when the men woke.

The bacon was about done when Tara turned to Amelia and grinned. "Hey, thanks for the show last night."

She couldn't help but bring it up. It was incredibly hot to watch Fury play with Amelia in front of most of the group.

Amelia's mouth dropped open. "You saw it all?"

Tara chuckled. "No, Traeger picked me up and threw me over his shoulder before you orgasmed. But I've got to tell you, he was all over me, and it was so good."

"He's always all over you."

Tara nodded and smiled. "Yeah, you're right about that. It just added a little spice to it."

"I'm glad to be of service," Amelia said sarcastically, then grinned.

"Hey, I smell bacon," Bear said behind them, making Tara laugh.

"Yeah, I figured you'd be the first one in here." Amelia chuckled.

"Hey, I'm a growing boy."

"Lord, if you grow any more, we won't be able to get you through the door."

"Are you calling me fat, woman?"

Tara grinned at Amelia to see what she'd say.

Amelia snorted, making Tara laugh. "Seriously. I'm talking about your height. You're already six-six and you already have to duck coming in and out through doorways."

Tara laughed when Amelia warned him about eating all the bacon. He didn't care, and since he was so big, she surmised that very few of the guys would argue with him.

Her smile fell when Carlee walked into the

kitchen. She could tell the woman was already angry at something, and she rolled her eyes.

"What's up your ass?" Bear said with a growl.

"Fuck off," she hissed as she grabbed a cup of coffee and a handful of bacon, then walked off. At the doorway, she turned back. "I'll be seeing you," she said in a smug way that made Tara nervous.

She didn't know what to say to the bitch before she turned and left. God, when was that woman leaving?

A few hours later, Tara was making another batch of cookies when Amelia came into the kitchen with her purse.

"I'm heading to the store for a few things. Is there anything you need?"

Tara looked up from the bowl of cookie dough she was stirring. "Sugar."

Amelia grinned. "Already on my list. The guys go through the stuff like it's candy."

"Do you want me to go with you?" she asked.

"No, I won't be long."

"Who are you taking with you?" Tara asked.

"No one. Everyone's busy."

Tara felt sick to her stomach. "I don't like that. Fury is going to be pissed. You know the rule."

"If I don't go to the store now, we won't have any food for lunch or dinner."

Tara started to get anxious. She didn't like Amelia out by herself. "Can you wait a bit, and I'll go with you?"

"No one is going to mess with me in town. They all know who I am."

"I hope you're right. Be careful."

Amelia grinned. "I always am."

Chapter Twenty

Tara was just pulling another pan of cookies from the oven when a commotion in the living area caught her attention. She raced out into the big room and to see everyone upset.

"What's going on?" she asked the guys closest to her.

"Someone kidnapped Amelia in the grocery store parking lot."

Tara felt bile creep up her throat at the thought of her friend getting hurt. She had her hands over her mouth, and she knew she'd lost the color in her face because she felt faint.

"D ... do they have any idea who?"

Bear shook his head. "No, that's why Fury is going crazy."

She nodded as she watched Fury bark out orders and the men rush out. Tara caught the murderous look in Fury's eyes and knew whoever touched Amelia was going to die.

"What can I do?"

Bear shook his head. "Nothing for now. Just pray."

That she was definitely doing.

She grabbed Bear's arm. "Please tell me if you find out any information."

"I will. Don't worry, mama, we'll get her back."

Tara nodded, turned, and walked back into the kitchen. She sat down in one of the stools the men had brought in for them, covered her face, and wept.

The smell of something burning brought her back, and she rushed to pull the last pan of cookies from the oven. One look at them, and she knew they were burnt.

She turned and tossed them in the garbage.

She tried to keep her hands busy so she wouldn't go crazy. Every time one of the doors opened, she jerked her head up. An hour crawled by. She washed all the dishes and then started on some brownies.

Rage came through the back door.

"Does Traeger know what happened?" she asked the man.

"Yeah, he's with Fury. They are going to get Amelia."

"Oh, God, where is she?"

"With Striker."

"Oh, my God," she cried out. "Isn't he in a rival gang?"

"Yes, but it's actually a good thing. He won't let anything happen to her because he knows we'd kill them all."

"But she's not hurt?"

"No." Rage grinned. "The last time I saw Fury, he was smiling."

Tara's shoulders drooped in relief. "Thank you."

Rage waved as he walked into the other room.

She sat on the stool and cried again, but this time in happiness. She was so thankful Amelia was okay, and that Fury would be bringing her home soon. A sigh of relief left her before she stood and finished making the brownies. They would use them to celebrate that night.

Another commotion had her running into the room. A happy cry burst from her mouth as Amelia came through the door. She was in front of her within a second and pulled her in her arms.

"Oh, thank God. I was so worried."

"I'm sorry. I hate that everyone was upset."

"Do they know who it was?"

"It was Carlee."

Tara's mouth dropped open. "What? How?"

Amelia looked at her and mouthed, "I'll tell you later."

Tara gave another hug and whispered, "Okay."

Fury grabbed ahold of Amelia. "She's going to our room until I come to get her."

Fury raised a brow when Amelia went to argue with him. Tara hid her smile and watched as Fury smacked Amelia's ass to get her moving up the stairs to their room.

She didn't envy Amelia. She'd broken one of the stricter rules Fury and Traeger had for them. Her friend would probably have a hard time sitting down the next day.

Tara turned toward the kitchen. If she was going to do everything herself, she needed to get started right away.

"Hey, Tara."

Tara turned at the door to the kitchen to face three of the club whores.

"Hey, what do you need?" No matter how they acted, Tara wasn't going to stoop to their level, so she was always friendly and courteous.

"Well," the one named Harper said and looked to the other two women. "We would like to help you if you need it."

Tara tried not to let her shock show. "Sure, that would be great." She turned to the kitchen when she caught sight of the two harder women who always gave Amelia and her problems. The three who wanted to help had always just stayed back and followed the other ones around.

She put them and Harley, who had stood in the background most of the time, to work cutting vegetables and stirring. Fortunately, someone had gone to get the things on their grocery list, or it would have been next to impossible to make a full meal.

Tara picked up the tray she'd made for Amelia.

"I'm going to run this up to Amelia. Why don't you start putting everything out like we usually do?"

"We got this," Sandra, another club whore, said and smiled.

Tara knocked on the bedroom door.

"Hi." Amelia stepped back.

Tara grinned. "Fury said I could bring you some dinner, but I can't stay and talk."

Amelia smiled. "Of course not. I'm in timeout."

Tara set the tray on the dresser and turned toward her.

Tears filled her eyes when she thought about the day. She squeezed Amelia as her arms came around her.

"I'm so sorry I scared everyone. I should have listened to you when you told me to take someone with me."

"I think we both learned a lesson today. I don't want you to worry about the kitchen. A few guys already went to the store, and a few of the whores and Harley are helping in the kitchen."

Tara was glad that made Amelia smile.

"Oh, the list was in my purse. I hope they got everything we needed… Oh, my God, where's my purse?"

"We got it back from the cop that found it."

Amelia exhaled in relief. "Thank you for being here, Tara."

"Always." Tara was feet from the kitchen when she caught the end of the three women's conversation, and they all stopped talking when she came in.

"What's up?" She looked at each of them.

"We were talking about what we thought would

be happening to Carlee," Sandra said.

"Like what?" Tara wasn't an idiot. She knew the woman would die that night. She had threatened and wanted to kill Fury's old lady.

"They'll torture her."

Tara's eyes widened. "What? Why? Why can't they just put a bullet in her brain?"

Harper shrugged. "The guys talk and forget we're around sometimes. Burn said when they got their hands on Carlee, they'd take her to the warehouse, wherever that is, and torture her until she apologizes."

Tara exhaled. "That's good."

Tiffany shook her head. "No. We got to know her. She was a class-A bitch. She'll hold out and razz them."

"But if they're hurting her, she'll shut up."

Harper looked at the women and shrugged. "We don't think she'll do that. I always thought there was something wrong with her brain. She never knew when to stop."

Tara pressed a hand against her mouth. She didn't want to imagine what they were doing to the woman. She realized Carlee deserved to die, but the torture? She didn't want to think about Traeger doing it.

Tiffany reached out and placed a hand on her arm. "Don't let it bother you. It's part of living here. As long as you don't betray them and you act halfway decent, you're good."

Tara heard the words Tiffany didn't say. If she screwed up, Traeger wouldn't save her? The thought made her stomach ache.

Before she could say anything, the guys started to come in for dinner.

She turned her attention to the men, glad to get her mind off what she'd just learned, but her thoughts kept going back to the question of Traeger hurting her.

Could he love her and still do that?

Harley walked back into the kitchen. Tara didn't want the woman to know any of this. She was still a little fragile and trying to settle in. She actually spent more time in her room than with the whole family.

Chapter Twenty-One

Tara lay on her side, facing away from the door and listening as Traeger came to bed that night. She hadn't been able to sleep because every time she closed her eyes, she saw Carlee screaming in pain.

She flinched away when she felt his hand on her shoulder.

"What's that about?" he asked.

She rolled to her back to see if she could see a difference in his face after seeing a woman being hurt.

"She's dead?"

Traeger narrowed his eyes. "What's going on?"

"How do you feel about me?"

"I fucking love you. You know this. You're kind of freaking me out."

"I just heard something tonight that made me think."

"Like what?" Traeger lay down beside her and propped his head on his pillow.

He looked relaxed, but she could see the stiffness of his muscles. She really wasn't trying to freak him out, but she wanted to know something, and she was afraid to ask because she didn't think she would like the answer.

"If I betrayed the club, I would die, right?"

"Fuck, babe, that will never happen."

"I know. I love you too much. But, if I did, would you do it?"

He cursed and then growled. "I don't want to fucking talk about this."

"Just answer the question."

"Hell, no. I couldn't do it," he shouted.

She exhaled and relaxed. "That's all I needed to know."

He cupped her cheek and studied her eyes, but she knew he could barely see her. The room was in different shades of darkness, except for the light from the streetlamp.

"I don't ever, and I mean ever, want to talk about this with you again. I love you."

She nodded. She was relieved by his answer. If he had told her he would have been the one, that he could actually look into the eyes of someone he loved and end their life, it would have destroyed something in her, and she'd question his feelings.

Her hand came up and caressed his face. "Never again. I just needed to know."

He bent and softly kissed her. "Now, you know. And now I need to fuck you until you can't walk."

She smiled and then gasped when he rolled on top of her, spread her legs, and thrust into her.

"Fuck. Please tell me you were ready for me."

She wrapped her legs around his waist. "I'm always ready for you."

He grinned, bent his head, and took her mouth with a passion that curled her toes. Simultaneously, one of his hands cupped her full breast, and he tormented her nipple.

"I don't like that you fucked with my head."

She tried to pull him in so she felt every inch of him. She whimpered. "Please. I'm sorry."

His thrusts got stronger, giving her what she needed. She had to arch her back to be able to take all of him.

When he pulled out of her and flipped her to her stomach, she gasped. He positioned her for his penetration, lifted her hips, and stuffed a pillow underneath her hips.

"After that little talk, I need your total submission.

You know what I'm saying?"

A shiver raced down her spine. "Yes. You want to fuck my ass."

"Yes. Let me know if I hurt you. I'll try to go slow."

She fisted the blanket by her head and relaxed her body. She was always apprehensive when he first started to work his cock into her ass, but once he got in, she always had the strongest orgasms.

It shocked her when Traeger plunged into her cunt a few times when she expected him in her ass.

He pulled out, fit the head of his cock to her puckered opening, and started to slide into her. He was so gentle the first time he pushed into that sensitive area of her body. But after he was in, he rode her hard every time.

She screamed when he thrust the last few inches into her. Tara concentrated on staying relaxed.

He bent forward. "Are you doing okay, baby?" he said against her ear.

She nodded. "Yes."

"Good."

He gently pulled out of her ass and suddenly thrust into her until she took his whole cock. Then he rode her hard for a few moments and felt him reach under her and pinch her clit.

"Come for me, baby. I'm not going to last."

A coiling pressure grew and grew until it burst inside of her, making one scream after another echo off the walls. Then she felt his cum fill her ass as he pumped into her.

It seemed like it took forever before he stopped fucking her. Only when his cock had softened did he stop. She collapsed when he let go of her hips. A wince twisted her face as he pulled out abruptly.

"Shit, I'm sorry, baby," he murmured and pressed a kiss to her lower back. "I'm going to get cleaned up. I'll be right back."

She patted his leg as she settled against the mattress. She knew the drill. Traeger would clean her up before he put her where he wanted her, wrapping himself around her and sleeping. The first few times he did, it had embarrassed her horribly. Now, she appreciated his care.

He got her situated on her side with her back against this chest. She felt him stick his nose in her hair and breathe her in.

"Fuck, babe. I love you so much it scares me."

She patted the hand that lay on her stomach. "You've got me until the end of time. I love you, and I can't see myself anywhere else but with you."

"You better not, or your ass will be a deep shade of red."

She snorted. "Way to kill a mood."

He chuckled. "Oh, you want a mood?" He rolled her to her back and slid on top of her. "I'll give you a mood," he whispered as he slid inside of her, making her sigh.

She was exactly where she was supposed to be—under him.

The End

DEVIL'S SONS MC: VOLUME ONE

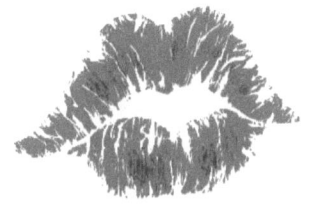

EVERNIGHT PUBLISHING ®

www.evernightpublishing.com